AROUND CHI-TOWN

Will the Connellys ever cease to amaze?

As Chicagoans primped for the society event of the season, blushing bride Alexandra Connelly wasn't dreaming of her walk down the aisle; she was apparently planning her escape route. On the eve of her near-million-dollar nuptials, the heiress was nowhere to be seen, stranding a flock of white doves and standing up a few hundred guests. Not even scion Grant Connelly knew where the bride-*not*-to-be had gone.

Paparazzi claim she's now licking her wounds across the Atlantic in brother Daniel's kingdom of Altaria, where the azure seas and cloudless skies are warming her frozen heart. Rumor has it that the immensely eligible Prince Phillip of Silverdorn is doing his share of heating up the runaway heiress. The two have been spotted in numerous tête-à-têtes around the picturesque island. Is Phillip catching Alexandra on the rebound, or making his own play?

Meanwhile, back on the home front, Grant Connelly is again making news, having hired two private investigators to look into the dealings at his corporation. Seems the Connellys are up to their eyeballs in mysteries on *both* sides of the Atlantic....

Dear Reader,

What could be more satisfying than the sinful yet guilt-free pleasure of enjoying six new passionate, powerful and provocative Silhouette Desire romances this month?

Get started with *In Blackhawk's Bed*, July's MAN OF THE MONTH and the latest title in the SECRETS! miniseries by Barbara McCauley. *The Royal & the Runaway Bride* by Kathryn Jensen—in which the heroine masquerades as a horse trainer and becomes a princess—is the seventh exciting installment in DYNASTIES: THE CONNELLYS, about an American family that discovers its royal roots.

A single mom melts the steely defenses of a brooding ranch hand in *Cowboy's Special Woman* by Sara Orwig, while a detective with a secret falls for an innocent beauty in *The Secret Millionaire* by Ryanne Corey. A CEO persuades a mail-room employee to be his temporary wife in the debut novel *Cinderella & the Playboy* by Laura Wright, praised by *New York Times* bestselling author Debbie Macomber as "a wonderful new voice in Silhouette Desire." And in *Zane: The Wild One* by Bronwyn Jameson, the mayor's daughter turns up the heat on the small town's bad boy made good.

So pamper the romantic in you by reading all six of these great new love stories from Silhouette Desire!

Enjoy!

Joan Marlow Golan

Joan Marlow Golan
Senior Editor, Silhouette Desire

Please address questions and book requests to:
Silhouette Reader Service
U.S.: 3010 Walden Ave., P.O. Box 1325, Buffalo, NY 14269
Canadian: P.O. Box 609, Fort Erie, Ont. L2A 5X3

The Royal &
the Runaway Bride
KATHRYN JENSEN

Published by Silhouette Books
America's Publisher of Contemporary Romance

Special thanks and acknowledgment are given to
Kathryn Jensen for her contribution to the
DYNASTIES: THE CONNELLYS series.

This book is for you, my loyal readers.
Thank you, thank you, thank you for your constant and
exuberant support! May love and light fill your hearts.

Kathryn

 SILHOUETTE BOOKS

ISBN 0-373-76448-0

THE ROYAL & THE RUNAWAY BRIDE

thing as natural as gravity and just as impossible to resist yet far more difficult to understand.

A stone balcony off the rear of the palace dropped away in wide steps to a formal garden, baking under Mediterranean heat even as the July sun set that evening. Sculpted shrubs formed arches, a maze and screens for the rose garden, interspersed with statues collected by the royal family over generations. Phillip wondered if the American clan was accustomed to such grandeur, then remembered the gossip that the Connellys were one of the wealthiest families in their own country. He caught a glimpse of emerald fabric whipping around a corner of hedgerow that separated the stables and yard from the prettily manicured greenery.

"Hey, you there, wait up!" he called, breaking into a run.

But if she heard, his shout had no effect. When he emerged from the shrubs to stand at the edge of the exercise yard, there was no sign of the less-than-daintily shod damsel in what had appeared to be Doc Martens. He caught the eye of a stable boy who was leading a chestnut mare across the yard.

"Did you see a young woman in a ball gown come this way?" Phillip asked in Italian.

The boy shook his head and kept going.

A low whinny and snort caught Phillip's attention, and he whipped around, moving toward the sound like a cat stalking its prey. Ducking into the dark interior of the stable at the third doorway, he waited for his eyes to adjust to the sudden lack of light, then looked down the long aisle strewn with sweet-smelling straw. She stood on the lowest rail of a stall, reaching over to stroke the nose of a pure white horse. Her attention was so fixed on the animal, she didn't react to his approach.

"Does the stable master know you're messing about with one of his most valued mounts?" he asked.

She jumped and snapped her hand back but recovered quickly, tipping her nose into the air. Her green eyes flashed defiantly at him. "Of course. He asked me to look in on him."

"He did, did he?" Phillip grinned, even more curious about her now. From a distance, she'd been intriguing. Up close she was dazzling, with a delicious hint of recklessness. "And why would he do that?"

"Because I'm...I'm a trainer. He asked me to work with—" Her gaze shifted almost imperceptibly to the bronze plaque on the stall's half door. "—with King's Passion."

"A trainer," he repeated, thinking that might well account for her mixed attire and uneasiness in a formal setting. His own trainer would do just about anything to avoid socializing with Phillip's friends. Although why, as a mere employee, she should be included at all in the celebration wasn't clear. "You're an American."

"Yes," she said, hopping backward off the rail. Her narrow shoulders settled firmly and her long, elegant neck straightened until she was looking him in the eye. "I work for the Connellys but came as a favor to lend a hand at the royal stable for the celebration."

"I see," he said. "So you've had a lot of experience with horses."

"Oodles." She flashed him a cocky grin.

He walked around her, checking out her physique without hiding his intent. Her shoulders and arms looked strong enough for the job, and she was slender, lightweight as a jockey, and seemed to be coordinated. He guessed she'd look damn fine straddling one of his jumpers. The image excited him. He could see her taking a five-foot rail on his favorite gelding.

"It's hard to find a good trainer these days," he commented.

She shrugged, still looking more interested in the white horse than in him as she stroked the patch of pink flesh between the animal's flaring nostrils.

"I have a problem horse in my own stable. Maybe you could break free of your duties here long enough to come over and take a look at him."

Her brows knit. "Oh, well…I would of course, but I'm terribly busy here. And I expect I won't be staying all that long."

"Too bad. I would have paid you well." No reaction. "And treated you to a fine lunch. My cook makes a bouillabaisse to die for."

Now her pretty eyes widened. Good, he thought. He'd found a weakness. Food.

"I really don't think I could—"

"Tell you what—" he stopped suddenly. "I didn't catch your name."

"Alex—" She seemed to hesitate, then said again, "Alex."

"Well, Alex, I'll speak to our king before the end of the evening. Perhaps we can spring you for a few hours tomorrow or the next day. I'm sure he won't mind. Besides, he owes me a favor."

"Oh?" Her gaze finally swerved from horse to man.

"I'll tell you about it sometime," he promised with a wink. "So it's a deal? You give my jumper a quick inspection, and I'll treat you to the finest seafood concoction in the Mediterranean."

She sighed, still looking unsure. "Agreed. But all I can spare is an hour or two at most." She was studying him for the first time, and he felt as if she suddenly had him under a magnifying glass. What was she looking for? he wondered. Or was she afraid of agreeing to take a side job?

"Are you always so serious about accepting work?" He was delighted to see her eyes soften when they at last met his. For once he allowed genuine warmth to enter his own expression. After all, she was safe, not some husband-hunting debutante or social climber. Just a working gal. The more she resisted his invitation, the better he felt about spending time with her.

She blinked at him and the corners of her lips lifted tentatively. "Not always." She crossed one booted foot over the other, still considering him. "Make it tomorrow. Early afternoon. You don't have to ask Daniel Connelly for permission. I'm free to make my own decisions where my time is concerned."

"Good, I'll send someone for you around one o'clock, if that's good for you. We'll make it a late luncheon after you see my problem child. That way you'll have the whole morning to work here."

"Yes," she agreed, her eyes skittering away from his. "I do want to make sure I finish up at the palace first."

Alexandra kicked herself all the way back to the ball-room. What had possessed her to accept Phillip Kinrowan's invitation to his estate? Sheer hunkiness, that was it! From the moment he was announced at the ball, she decided he was the handsomest man she'd ever laid eyes on.

And, on top of his looks, he owned a stable full of horses.

From the time she'd been a little girl, she'd adored the creatures. Unfortunately, they didn't always return her affection—unless you could count as tokens of endearment all those bruises and fractures she'd suffered during lessons when she was a schoolgirl. Among the Connellys' social set, proper English riding lessons were a must. As crucial an element of her education as knowing how to read the New York Stock Exchange quotes in the *Chicago Sun-Times* financial section, according to Grant Connelly, her father. She didn't hold her failures against the horses. Under most circumstances, she hadn't done badly at all. It was just that once in a while she seemed to develop a slippery bottom, and there she'd be on the ground, studying clouds. She could never be described as a polished horsewoman.

So, what had possessed her to tell Kinrowan that she was a trainer? A childhood fantasy, perhaps? It might have been all right if he hadn't immediately asked for her help. Then her pride hadn't let her admit the fib. She'd have to show up at his place and pretend to be knowledgeable. If she kept the visit short, Alexandra reasoned, she should be all right. Surely she knew enough about horses to fake her way through an hour or two of horse-related conversation.

Alexandra shook her head, lifted her skirts and clomped in her favorite boots up the wide marble steps from the garden to the patio. Well, it would be a kick anyway. And a man who obviously had no interest in her other than professionally, and probably had tons more money than Daddy, couldn't possibly hold the usual threat men had been to her. What the hell... Maybe an afternoon with Phillip Kinrowan would help her forget. Help her start to wash away the terrible pain, and stop thinking about the reason she'd run away from Chicago, from her friends and the most bitter disappointment of a young woman's life.

The next morning the castle was quiet. Her brother, Daniel, and his wife, Erin, were breakfasting late on the veranda. She approached in her trademark Doc Martens, khaki hiking shorts and an oversized jersey. "You'd think after all that food last night, I wouldn't be hungry," she commented, sitting down and in one motion reaching for a plate of pastries.

Erin smiled at her. "I think we burned the banquet food off with all that dancing. I saw you on the floor with a dozen different men."

Alex shrugged. "It was an okay party, I guess."

"Leave it to Alex to understate any situation," Daniel said, shaking his head. "A ball held in my honor at a castle, and my little sister says it was an okay party." He laughed affectionately.

"Well, it was," she objected, giving his cheek a sisterly pinch. "I mean, it isn't as if Daddy hasn't invited half of Chicago to celebrate every new business coup he makes."

"I seem to recall one little girl's birthday party that included pony rides and a half-dozen clowns hired from Ringling Brothers."

Daniel was making fun of her and she hated it. If he was implying that she was in any way spoiled, he was wrong. It was just that when you grew up in a family like the Connellys it was hard to know how to live other than in luxury. Money had never been an issue, until she'd become an adult. Then she'd learned its power as well as its curses.

For the last several years all she'd known, in fact, were the curses. They'd kept her from feeling satisfied with herself, happy with her friends. More than anything, money had gotten in the way of her finding love. She might have grown up with a silver spoon in her mouth but she'd always believed in the basic honesty of people, particularly two people who cared deeply for each other. Until the day before her wedding, she'd thought that Robert loved her, because he had said he did and he'd acted as if he did. She'd even been able to ignore her brother Justin's warnings about Robert a few days before. But then she'd overheard her fiancé's conversation with Jessy Weintraub, her maid of honor. And her world had fallen apart.

"He's kidding, right?" Erin asked. "Ringling Brothers' clowns?"

"I'm afraid not. Our father likes to do things in a big way, in case you haven't yet noticed. Money has never been known to hold Grant Connelly back." But it had held *her* back. If she couldn't find love, the very least she should have been able to find was herself. She hadn't succeeded. She still wondered who Alexandra Connelly really was. Why had she been put on this planet? What was the special gift she had been meant to share with the world?

Or was she just another rich girl destined to marry wisely, chair committees for charities…and wish she were someone else?

So far, all she had discovered was that she was good at attracting men. Like Robert Marsh. Men who were intelligent, good-looking, aggressive at both work and play. In short, every woman's dream. Every woman but her. Because these men all saw the same thing in her—a fast road toward wealth and success. When your father was the famous Grant Connelly, any man who married you was guaranteed a place in Connelly Corporation and a niche in a family that liked to share its prosperity.

For a moment, there was a vision of white silk and a beaded bodice, of a veil that had covered her face to hide tears on the day before her wedding. It had been during the final fitting that she'd walked in on her fiancé and best friend. The rest was a blur as she flung off shreds of priceless fabric, sobbing as she told herself she would fly to the

Virgin Islands, to China, or to the most remote regions of Africa that very night. And, *no,* she would not be marrying Robert. Ever!

She had left him, if not literally at the altar, only hours away from it.

Bitterness and anger seethed within her again, subsiding only as she sipped a cool tropical juice drink. She should have seen the signs, should have learned over the years. The world was full of Robert Marshes, and the only way to have a safe relationship with a man was, ironically, by lying to him.

Thus she would be a horse trainer if that was what she chose to be for a few hours.

Phillip Kinrowan's estate perched on a cliff overlooking the blue-green Tyrrhenian Sea. The day was bright and warm. The stone had baked in the sun all morning and felt smooth and pleasantly hot against the soles of Alex's bare feet as she climbed. She squinted up the steep face of the cliff, then looked back down to the beach where the motor launch had left her, its driver pointing toward the ancient stairway. Above her she could see nothing but blue sky. The smell of wild jasmine and portulaca was almost overpowering, a heady brew when mixed with the brine of the ocean lapping at the rocks beneath her.

At last her head rose above the edge of the cliff and a long, low white structure came into view, set back from the rocks by a carpet of manicured emerald grass. She drew in a slow breath. "Oh, my..."

It wasn't the largest house she'd ever seen, but it had character and charm and something that didn't come from one or two generations of luck and money. This place had old-world history built into it. It might have been constructed of the gleaming white limestone in the days when

Rome or Athens was devouring chunks of Europe. Or it might have been built centuries later to emulate the classic lines of antiquity. Slender white columns stretched up to support a portico of sun-catching stone. Long wings of the low building curved around a fountain, a circular drive, and a beautifully maintained garden. She judged that although there was only one floor, the house could accommodate fifty or more overnight guests within its many sun-drenched rooms.

Feeling less confident about her quick visit, she slowly walked up the path of crushed shells toward the main entrance of the estate. Before she reached the steps, a figure in a white shirt and pants, a straw Panama hat and leather espadrilles moved out of the shadows and came down the steps toward her.

Phillip smiled. "Welcome to my home, Sandora."

"Have you been lurking there waiting for long?" she asked.

"The launch jockey radioed that he'd dropped you off on the beach."

"I see. When you said you'd send someone to pick me up in Altaria-Ville, I assumed it would be a car."

"It could have been, but it would have taken longer. And the view by water can't be beat." He held out a hand to her, and she assumed he was either going to shake hands American-style, or kiss her fingertips as Europeans do. Instead he enclosed her fingers in a warm grip and tucked them between his elbow and the side of his body, then began walking her across the lawn toward what she could now see was the stables.

"Well," she said nervously, "the view *was* great. Thank you."

"My pleasure. Lunch won't be ready for an hour. I hope you don't mind looking at Eros first."

"Eros?" The god of love, if she remembered her mythology. Another name for Cupid, the imp who had caused Medea to fall in love with Jason while on his search for the golden fleece. The outcome had been tragic.

"My problem horse. He's always been a wonderful mount. Won me a bundle of Grand Prix ribbons as a jumper. Aside from that, I just plain like him better than any other horse in my stable. But he's refusing jumps now."

"When did he start doing that?" she asked.

"About a month ago. It happened very suddenly. No warning at all. One of my exercise lads was taking him through his paces, just warming him up easy before I came out to ride for the day. By the time I reached the ring, the lad was on the ground cursing the horse, and Eros was in a lather, pacing the yard as if he'd been terribly frightened."

"He might have been. You can never tell with horses what will spook them." She felt satisfied with how astute and experienced she sounded. "Did you ask the boy what had happened?"

"Of course." Phillip anxiously dragged fingers through his thick brown hair. "No one in the yard saw anything that might have scared the animal. Nothing out of the ordinary seems to have happened during those few minutes."

"Hmmm," Alex said, aiming for an expression of sage perplexity. "Well, let's take a look at him."

Phillip led her down a row of half doors, the generous-sized stalls behind them smelling of cedar chips, saddle soap and the natural muskiness of horseflesh. She had always loved this part of being around horses—the smells, rough and masculine textures, sounds of hooves restlessly shifting on wooden planks, snuffles and whinnies of horses talking to one another in their secret language. It was the riding part that hadn't been as easy, or at least as painless.

Phillip stopped in front of a stall and whistled between his teeth. Almost immediately, an enormous black head with shining dark eyes appeared in the opening. "Hello, Eros, old man," Phillip murmured tenderly. He ran a gentle hand beneath the horse's chin and thumped the side of its neck.

"Phillip," she gasped, "he's gorgeous." She meant it.

Her eyes took in the dark line of the animal's body on the other side of the door. The classic lines of the Thoroughbred were perfected in the shining flanks, the delicate limbs and well-muscled barrel chest of the horse. She'd ridden some wonderful horses as a girl, up until the time she'd quit her lessons fourteen years ago when she turned sixteen and gotten up the nerve to tell her father riding just wasn't for her. But Eros made them all look like commoners.

Alex swallowed over a lump of emotion in her throat. Would she ever dare ride such a horse? Or course, Phillip probably didn't let just anyone hop on the back of this magnificent creature, clearly his pride and joy.

"Any opinion?" he asked, interrupting her admiration.

"He's wonderful, of course," she breathed.

"I meant, your professional judgment."

"Oh. Of course." She recovered quickly, her mind racing to come up with something...anything that might sound like trainer-talk. "Ummm. Well, anyone can see he's still jittery. Something has broken his confidence."

Phillip scowled and reached out to rest his palm over the wide, velvety bridge of Eros's nose. "You can see that in here? Just by looking at him?"

She nodded wisely. "Yes. I've seen this sort of thing a

lot. The whole character of the horse can change after one bad incident.''

''But nothing happened to—''

''Nothing your stable hands will admit to,'' she said quickly. ''I don't know about you, but people who work for my fa— my employer,'' she corrected herself hastily, ''although they may be loyal and honest in most ways, often have trouble admitting to a mistake. They don't want to make their boss angry, so it's natural to cover up, hoping things will mend themselves.''

He studied her for a long moment. ''I suppose you're right. I probably will never know what, if anything, got to Eros that day.''

''Exactly.'' She felt more confident now that she'd gotten him to agree with her, even though her point was a vague one at best. ''So all we can do now is build the horse's confidence.''

''How do we do that?''

She only had to think for a second before she remembered how she'd recovered after a few bad falls. ''You start at the beginning. Retrain him as if he's never jumped before.''

Phillip shook his head. ''My own trainer said that he must be made to take a couple of high jumps, then he'll be fine.''

She let out a doubtful chortle. ''Right. And how are you going to force a couple thousand pounds of horseflesh over a five-foot hurdle, short of using a forklift?''

He smiled and stepped closer to her, their shoulders touching, and she felt a tingle of excitement. ''You have a point. Tell me more,'' he said.

She let Eros sniff her palm then stroked his sleek black throat. ''Ride him on the flat for a dozen or more loops around the ring. No jumps at all. Then walk him over a rail lying on the ground. After he's comfortable with that, move up to a rail placed no more than four or five inches off the ground. Keep raising the height slowly, but don't move him up until he takes the new level without hesitation. If it takes weeks, fine. Don't push him.''

Phillip nodded slowly. "It sounds logical. You've used this technique before with other horses?''

"Zillions!'' She smiled when Eros playfully nuzzled her cheek. And now, she thought, time for lunch. She couldn't get enough of the wonderful Mediterranean seafood found all over the island.

But Phillip had other ideas. "Let's get him saddled.''

"What?'' She stared at him apprehensively.

"No time like the present. Besides, you yourself said you won't be here for long. I want to take advantage of your expertise.''

"But I'm sure your own trainer—''

"He hasn't succeeded yet, and I don't want to take the chance that Eros might connect Marco with whatever originally spooked him. He seems to like you. Maybe a woman's touch is what he needs.''

"I haven't brought riding gear,'' she objected.

"There's plenty you can use in the tack room. Just down there.'' He pointed. "I keep spare boots, crops and such for guests. What shoe size do you take?''

"Six, American,'' she said wearily.

"I'm sure there's something that will fit you. Go along. I'll get him ready for you.''

Great, she thought glumly a moment later as she pulled riding breeches over her casual shorts and wedged her feet into leather riding boots. What was she going to do now? She could confess to Phillip Kinrowan that she had lied to him and wasn't who she claimed to be. But that would be humiliating. She didn't care if he was angry, but she wouldn't be laughed at.

Or she could call his bluff and ride Eros. *And risk breaking your neck by doing so,* a little voice inside her warned.

But the timid jumper had seemed as gentle as a lamb in his stall. Sure, Thoroughbreds were unpredictable and their moods could change without warning. But she knew how to handle a basic trot around a ring or a walkover exercise, and that was all she was going to do. She'd explain to Phillip that pressing the horse to take a jump of any height today would be premature and could permanently ruin him for competition. What owner would take that risk?

Alex grinned. She could do this. No sweat. Then on to bouillabaisse!

Phillip cinched up Eros's saddle, talking comfortingly to him all the while. "She weighs hardly more than a feather, old man. You won't feel her. And you saw how nice she was, right? Pretty woman like that, she'd never do anything to hurt you. Just relax and take her for a little spin around the ring, and let me enjoy the view, huh? Do that for me?"

It seemed almost too good to be true, Alex's advice. He wondered why such common sense hadn't occurred to him or Marco. So simple. Start from the beginning. But she was obviously well experienced. He was excited to see how Alex would handle Eros. The horse was spirited, true, but he had been a well-mannered mount until the day he started refusing jumps.

Phillip walked Eros into the yard, toward the largest of the training rings. Two of his stable boys were talking to a man he recognized as being from the royal court. He wondered if he'd been sent with a message for Alex and hoped there wasn't a reason to take her back to the palace before they'd had time for a leisurely lunch. He was about to ask but Alex appeared, jogging across the yard, her cheeks prettily flushed.

"Is he ready?"

"He's all yours," Phillip said, handing over the reins to her. "Need a leg up?"

She shook her head, wedged a toe into a stirrup and lightly bounced once to propel herself up and into the English-style saddle. "Piece of cake."

"So I see." He chuckled. She really did look sexy up there astride the big horse. He hadn't guessed wrong about that. "What's next?"

"We won't do much more than get to know each other," she said. "Just cruise a couple of times around the ring. If he's happy with that and wants more, I'll step him across a few rails."

"Signal me if you want them and I'll set up for you," he offered.

She nodded, clucked once at Eros and touched him lightly on his flank with her crop. He responded by walking smoothly toward the ring. Phillip watched as she moved Eros into a relaxed canter, sitting erect and easily on his back. They looked a perfect match, although he was a large horse for such a small woman. Still, temperaments often counted for more than size where horses were concerned.

"That's quite an animal you have there," a voice said, speaking in the local Italian dialect.

Phillip turned to face a man he recognized from Daniel's court. He was reed thin, with a slightly receding hairline and a no-nonsense expression. "Yes. One of my favorites. I'm lucky to have come across such an experienced trainer at a time when I need one."

"Oh? Who is that?"

Phillip tilted his head toward Alex. "She's riding him now."

There was a pause that Phillip read as confusion. He looked at the stranger. "Is something wrong?"

"No, nothing at all." But the man seemed cautious of the words he chose next. "I'm Gregor Paulus. I was Prince Marc's assistant, before the accident." The two men shook hands. "I'm the one responsible for seeing to the comfort and travel arrangements of the American branch of the family and their staff while they're on the island. I have a message from the palace for the, um, the trainer."

"I hope she doesn't have to rush back. I've promised her lunch," Phillip explained.

Paulus smiled. "That's very good of you, sir. No, there's no rush."

"Perhaps I can give her the message?" Phillip asked.

"It's of a personal nature...from her family in the States. I'll just go back up to the house, if that's all right, and wait until she's finished."

"We won't be long," Phillip promised, then turned back to Alex.

"He's doing great!" she called out.

"I can see that." Phillip waved then grinned at the beautiful picture before him—woman and horse, moving in fluid motion as one.

"Ready for a step-over?" he called on her next loop.

"Sure, why not?" She beamed at him, looking as if she were thoroughly enjoying herself.

Phillip ducked through the fence and walked into the ring. He moved two rails from jump supports down to the ground, leaving nothing for Eros to clear above three inches. An easy step-over, just as Alex had described. Then he moved out of the way and leaned casually against the inside of the fence to watch.

Eros slowed as he approached the rails lying on the ground. Alex gently guided him over them. She leaned down to whisper in the horse's ear and hugged him around the neck. "Good job, boy." She waved at Phillip. "Once more?"

"Go for it." He gave her a thumbs-up for encouragement, then watched, transfixed, as Eros and his lovely rider made five more loops around the ring.

Alex was thrilled with herself. Her plan was working! Nothing to this training business, she thought. "Let's try a low jump!" she shouted at Phillip.

"Do you really think he's ready?" Phillip frowned. The last time Eros had balked with him in the saddle, he'd barely been able to hang on.

"Sure," she said. "I think he's up to a little challenge now. Set the jump low—just two feet off the ground." Since even a beginning jumper could easily clear four feet, this would be a piece of cake.

Phillip shrugged. After all, Alex was the pro and must know what she was doing. He walked to the middle of the ring and set the pole in the second notch from the ground. Eros's hoofbeats as he rounded the far curve of the ring accompanied Phillip as he returned to the gate, where he stood to watch. He studied Alex's face as she and her mount came around the bend and faced the jump.

Something stubborn and proud was reflected in her expression. She bit down on her bottom lip, leaned forward to say something in Eros's ear, then brought the huge animal into a smooth gallop. It was at that moment he saw the flicker of fear in Eros's dark eyes as they rolled in a panic at the sight of the jump. Phillip was suddenly terrified for Alex.

"No!" he shouted, knowing that no matter how good a rider she was, no matter how much Eros trusted her, the

animal's terror would get the better of him. They were
headed for disaster. "Alex, don't do it!"

But a wild fire shone in Alex's eyes and she ignored
him. Phillip wanted to close his eyes. He did hold his
breath. He gripped the fence on either side of him, and
time seemed to stand still as dust flew from beneath Eros's
hooves and the ground trembled and the horse sped past
him heading directly for the jump.

Alex leaned forward in the saddle, standing in the stirrups, her legs acting as springs, ready to absorb the impact
of landing on the other side of the rail. A few meters before
the jump, Eros balked, tossing his head and refusing to
take to air. His big body twisted and he wrenched himself
about, setting his hooves. Alex, unprepared for the sudden
stop, was helpless to retain her seat. Thrown over the
horse's head, she tumbled to the hard ground, landing with
a sickening crack.

Phillip's heart pounded in his chest. His eyes burned,
and for breathless seconds he couldn't make himself move.
Alex didn't move, either. Eros pawed the dust, whinnied
and danced nervously.

At last, a groom raced into the ring, grabbed the horse's
reins and led him away, looking at Phillip as if he must
be mad. As if he were to blame for the woman's recklessness! Others quickly gathered outside the rails, but no one
dared say a thing. "Alex!" he breathed, breaking out of
his paralysis and running to her.

Two

Alex's first awareness that anything had gone wrong was the sudden pressure of hard earth beneath her body, where a leather saddle had been moments earlier. She made herself lie absolutely still, not daring to move. It was a position she remembered with no fondness from her teenage years, the last time she'd seriously ridden. The last time she'd jumped.

She kept her eyes closed and, one body part at a time, assessed her condition. Her head—aside from a dull headache, it didn't feel bad. Thank goodness she'd worn a helmet. Her back—she gently contracted the muscles and felt her spine respond, straightening just a fraction of an inch but enough to reassure her that all was in working order. Her legs—she wiggled her toes and tightened the muscles in her legs. Her arms—well, the fingers could flex. She tried to push herself up onto one elbow now that things appeared to be functioning. A flash of white-hot pain sliced through her left shoulder.

"Ow!" she moaned and fell back down to the ground.

"Don't try to get up!" a masculine voice ordered. "Devon," Phillip shouted to one of his stable boys, "call Doctor Elgado. Tell him we need him immediately."

"What happened?" Alex asked foggily, honestly remembering nothing beyond the moment she'd come around the circle after taking Eros over the rails laid out on the ground.

"You missed a two footer."

She scowled and felt Phillip's hand slide gently beneath her head, pillowing it and raising it even with the line of her neck and spine. "Why'd I do a dumb thing like—" Then it came back to her. Her little deception. Horse trainer, indeed!

"I'm sorry, Alex. Dear God, I'm so sorry." Phillip's voice was choked with emotion. "I just assumed you knew best. I should never have let you try to jump him."

"He was doing so well…" she murmured, lapsing into a spell of dizziness.

"And you looked magnificent up there. Don't waste your strength trying to talk. Do you know where you're injured? Is it your back?"

"No, I think I'm okay there. But my shoulder, the one closest to your hand—"

His fingers softly kneaded the area around her shoulder blade, then forward in the soft hollow between her armpit and breast. She felt the area warm and tingle to his touch. Then she winced at the sudden sharp pain.

"Yes, there," she said tightly.

"Sorry, I didn't mean to hurt you. I can't tell if anything's broken. My physician will be here soon."

She nodded. The ring's dusty surface felt as hard as the

limestone cliff she'd climbed earlier that day. "Do you think we could wait somewhere more comfortable?"

"I don't want to move you if there's any chance of spinal injury."

"I'm sure there's not," she said. "Everything moves. No numbness anywhere, no pain except in the shoulder."

"You can't walk," he objected, "and if I try to carry you I might hurt you."

"This isn't exactly cozy down here," she said dryly. "Besides, you owe me, Prince."

"Yes, ma'am," he grumbled.

She opened her eyes to peek up at him as he carefully positioned himself over her and slipped one arm beneath her, taking care to support the injured shoulder against his chest as he rolled her toward him. When he lifted her, she felt a flash of raw fire in her shoulder and she squeezed her eyes shut. But she knew he was doing his best not to hurt her anymore. Once she was fully enclosed in his arms and he was standing erect, the pain lessened.

He carried her past rows of concerned faces as stable boys and household staff looked on.

"Someone ought to teach that horse the difference between up and down," she grumbled aloud. Relieved laughter from his staff rewarded her effort to lighten the atmosphere.

"Is there anything I can do, sir?" a woman in an apron asked worriedly.

"Have Juan wait at the gate for the doctor and bring him straight to the parlor. Mint tea might be nice," he added vaguely.

"Brandy would be nicer," said Alex. "In a very big glass."

The woman chuckled. "Brave girl. Brandy she is." She cast Phillip a chastising glare. "Why you not warn her?"

"I did—I did!" He let explanations go on a long sigh.

Alex said nothing more until he had laid her down on a long, soft settee arranging pillows beneath her head and neck to support her. Pulling up a leather hassock, he sat close beside her, holding her hand between his two and bringing her fingertips to his bowed forehead as he closed his eyes tightly and muttered something to himself.

"What was that?" Alex asked.

"I'm sorry. I'm so very— I know Eros better than you. I should never have let you take him past a simple canter. It's just that you'd convinced me that you were on the right track. All that talk about Eros's fears, starting at the beginning, building his confidence."

"Well, it's what a rider does after she takes a fall so I figured why shouldn't it work with a horse?" He looked blankly at her. "I mean," she added hastily, "it's worked so well with other horses I've trained."

"You're a daring young woman." He shook his head and kissed her knuckles, his eyes wandering as he became lost in thought. She wondered if he was even aware of the intimacy of their position—he bending over her, his large hands enclosing her small one, his warm mouth lingering against the flesh of her curled fingers.

They stayed like that for a while longer, and she didn't move, didn't pull her hand away. Didn't even want to lose touch with him. She knew that it was guilt, keeping him here beside her. But she didn't mind as long as he stayed.

At last Phillip looked down at her and rolled his amber eyes in dismay. "How can I show you how sorry I am for this?"

She followed the line of his strong jaw with a lingering gaze. "Maybe I'll think of something," she murmured. He *was* incredibly handsome. Reckless, impulsive thoughts came to mind. Visions of his wide hands touching her in more intimate places. She felt a steamy flush wash over her entire body.

There was a commotion in the hallway outside the parlor and an older man in tropical casuals burst through the door and hastily crossed the room. He was carrying a small leather case and he immediately pushed Phillip aside to get close to Alex. "Your boy tells me the young lady took a bad fall."

"Yes, Doctor. She was on Eros."

"Couldn't you have found a more reliable mount for her?" he chided Phillip. "Last time you jumped him, it was a fiasco." Alex got the impression that the doctor must also be involved with European jumping to be so aware of the horse's problems.

"I'll explain later. Just look to her, will you?" Phillip snapped irritably.

Alex smiled, amused by his impatience. It was clear he was going to suffer through the disapproval of a lot of people for a long time because of her accident.

The doctor made everyone including Phillip leave the room while he opened her blouse and examined her shoulder, then he listened to her heart and checked her reflexes.

"Well?" she asked when he was done.

"You are in amazingly good shape for the spill you took, miss. But that shoulder is sprained. You'll need to wear a sling to rest it until it heals."

"How long will that take?" she asked.

He frowned, looking uncertain. "I'd give it a few weeks." He took supplies from his bag. "This might hurt a bit while I adjust the tension of the sling. Do you want Phillip back in the room to hold your hand?"

She thought for a moment. "No. A little more of this fine brandy will do." She took four very long swallows, draining the snifter. Immediately, a heady stream of warmth flowed through her throat, filling her chest and rushing out to the tips of her toes and fingers. She shut her eyes and braced herself. "Go for it, doc."

Phillip paced the vestibule while his housekeeper looked on worriedly. "Are you sure, sir, there is nothing I can—"

"Nothing, Maria. Thank you. Just go on with—" He waved a dismissing hand. "Whatever." No doubt she had been preparing their luncheon, which would never be eaten now.

Alone again, he stared helplessly at the closed door to the parlor. A single sharp cry of pain made him jump. He took three hasty steps toward the door, his hand reaching out for the knob. Then he stopped himself. The doctor had sent him out for good reason. He must respect Alex's right to privacy.

Phillip bit down on his lower lip so hard he tasted the salt of his own blood. The outside door opened.

It was Paulus. "I was taking a walk through your fine garden while I waited, and heard there had been an accident."

"Alex, yes. But she's all right. The doctor says it's a sprain." Phillip had been listening at the door, unable to wait for an official announcement.

"I'll call the palace and inform them."

"Yes," Phillip said, realizing that was probably something he should have been doing instead of all this useless pacing. "Thank you."

A moment later, the door still hadn't opened and Paulus returned. "King Daniel says I'm to bring her back with me as soon as the doctor says she is able to be moved."

"Oh." A shadow of dull, gray disappointment fell over Phillip. Why had he assumed Alex would remain here with him? "No," he said hastily.

"No?"

"It was my fault, the accident. I didn't warn her strongly enough. She should remain under my roof to recuperate."

The man hesitated. "I…well, that's not the king's wish. It isn't for me to say whether—"

"She'll stay here," Phillip stated, his mind made up. "I'll speak with King Daniel. She shouldn't be moved any more than is necessary." He didn't know that to be a fact, but it sounded a good enough reason. "I'm responsible for her condition, and I should see to her recovery."

Paulus looked puzzled but didn't argue further. "I will return to the palace with your message."

"I'll call as soon as I have my physician's report."

Phillip turned back toward the parlor door. It was quiet now inside. He hoped that was good news.

Alex was barely aware of the doctor leaving the room. The brandy had numbed her, and the pain in her shoulder had retreated to a dull ache as soon as the doctor finished messing with the sling. She nestled into the soft cushions of Phillip's settee and drifted off to sleep.

She floated.

For the first time in weeks Alex felt detached from the terrible disappointment that had chased her halfway around the world to her brother's new home, Altaria. She hadn't planned to attend the ball in his honor, but it had provided a welcome escape from her troubles.

She remembered Robert's words as he spoke to her friend Jessy and the cruel sound of his laughter, slurred by too much alcohol. "Love Alex? You've got to be kidding. But marrying her is well worth the sacrifice of my freedom in exchange for all I'll gain from Connelly Corporation."

She remembered every word as clearly as if he stood before her now, speaking them anew. Oh how she wished she'd listened to Justin's words of warning. *He* knew that Robert was a womanizer, that Robert was just using her. Why hadn't she seen the man for what he was? Tears filled her eyes as she slept.

A hand brushed the dampness from cheek. She blinked her eyes open.

Phillip bent over her, his honey-colored eyes concerned. "Is the pain bad?"

"No," she whispered.

"It hurts enough to cry."

She shook her head. "That's something else. I'm being silly. Never mind."

He frowned, obviously confused, but she wasn't about to explain her aborted wedding to him.

"I've arranged for you to stay here," he said.

"What?" She looked up at him, astonished. "Why would I want to do that?"

"You were injured on my property, so I'm responsible for your recovery. I intend to see to your care."

"I see. And that will soothe your conscience?"

"Conscience aside, it's only right."

"I don't know…" She tried to pull herself into a sitting position, but a sudden tightness in her shoulder promised pain she didn't want to feel and she settled back down against the pillows. "The doctor said I'll be fine walking around as long as I don't move this." She glanced sideways at her shoulder, resting in the white cotton sling. "He expects I'll be pretty much back to normal in a couple of weeks."

"I suppose you'd be more comfortable back in Chicago, in your own home."

Back at Lake Shore Manor, she thought dismally, her parents' home. Not in the house she had planned to share with Robert, before her dreams had shattered.

"I suppose," she murmured.

"Oh, I almost forgot. The palace aide left a note for you." He held out a folded piece of paper.

It was a telephone message taken by one of the palace secretaries in a pointy European-style script. It was from Robert. As she read it, ice crystals formed in her heart.

"Not bad news, I hope?" he asked.

Very bad news. Robert wanted her to come home. Robert wanted to explain his flirtation with Kimberly Lindgren and his disturbing comments to Jessy, to make things right, to try again and set a new date for the wedding.

Fat chance, buddy, she thought, tears nearly coming to her eyes again. She hadn't known him as well as she'd thought she did. Just well enough to realize that the words he'd spoken to her maid of honor the night before their wedding were from the heart and true to his character.

Robert didn't love her. Perhaps she'd sensed that from the start but refused to admit it to herself. She had so desperately wanted love, marriage, a family of her own, and there he was offering her these things in his oh-so-charming way. But he loved only what she could bring him—wealth, her father's power and influence, a future of success that depended little on his own effort or ingenuity.

And if she didn't return to Chicago, what then? He would come after her. She was certain of that much because he was a determined man. Without her, without their marriage, he had nothing but a midmanagement position with her father's company. That is, if Grant didn't fire him outright once she explained to her parents her sudden disappearance from Chicago. She hadn't yet found the strength to talk about her reasons for walking out on Robert on the eve of their wedding. Nor had she found the nerve to face Robert again. But she could at least make it difficult for him to find her until she was ready to face him.

"I'll stay," she said quickly.

"Really?" Phillip looked surprised after her earlier refusal.

"Yes," she said and slid him a playful smile. "If only to milk your guilt."

He grimaced. "It wasn't my intention that you fall!"

"I know that," she said, settling back against a fluffy pillow. "Still, if you should feel a teensy bit responsible you could bring me a cup of that wonderful smelling bouillabaisse you promised."

He grinned. "It's as good as done."

Phillip didn't know how long he could keep Alex in resting mode. She was like a little kid, constantly trying to find excuses to leave the couch when she was supposed to be quiet and not stress her shoulder. Although he could easily have asked his housekeeper or any one of the others on his staff to fetch things for her, he felt obligated to wait on her, personally. His employees found this highly entertaining, but he didn't care. He'd make sure she gave her shoulder a chance to heal if it killed him.

By the time he returned to the parlor on the third day of her stay, carrying a steaming cup of Earl Grey tea and a plump raisin scone, she was sitting on the edge of the settee.

"The doctor said you should rest. Lie down and I'll pour for you," he offered.

"I'm uncomfortable," she complained, pouting at him. "Too much of this lying around must be bad for the circulation. I want to go outside." She peered out the window. "It looks beautiful out there."

"Rest," he said.

"I could rest just as well on the chaise lounge on the terrace, I'll bet my shoulder would warm up in the sunshine and heal faster." She started to stand up.

He set the tray down with a sigh. "Very well, the terrace it is."

She laughed at him as he scooped her up in his arms and strode out the open French doors into the Mediterranean sunshine. He deposited her on a cushioned chaise and looked down at her. "Better?"

"Much," she said. "Thank you."

He smiled, pleased he'd been able to once more delay her restlessness.

"Wait here. I'll go get the tea."

When he returned, she had rearranged her thin white cotton robe worn over a sea-green bikini to bare her long legs. He drew a sharp breath at the tug in his loins. She was stunning—the contrast between her pale ivory skin and her cropped, black hair. Her emerald eyes flashed up at him. He gulped. Unable to say what was really on his mind, he blurted out, "Sunscreen. I forgot the sunscreen."

She shook her head at him. "Stop fussing over me. I'm fine."

She was a darn sight more than just fine, Phillip thought when he returned, drew up a chair beside hers, and watched her smooth lotion from her toes, over her ankles, then up her calves, thighs and hips. Lust curled up hot and ready inside of him. He didn't think he could risk staying with her any longer.

"If you're comfy now," he said, coughing to clear his suddenly tight throat, "I have some business I should attend to."

"You can't stay and keep me company?" she asked.

"If you want someone to talk to, I can send to the castle for someone."

"Most of the guests would have left by now," she said. "Besides, I don't like them."

"Any of them?"

She shrugged. "I don't like rich people."

He laughed. "I'm not exactly a pauper, woman, in case you haven't noticed."

"You're different," she said, smoothing another dollop of lotion across the flat of her stomach, then circling her fingertips around her belly button. He followed the sensuous motion of her fingers with fascination. "You don't put on airs and spend money for the thrill of it."

"How do you know so much about me?"

"I'm good at figuring out people." With one tragic exception, she thought, then chased that sad part of her life from her mind. Robert was no longer a concern. She had put him out of her life. "It's sort of a hobby of mine, studying people and, sometimes, pretending to be like them."

She tipped her head to one side and observed him, wondering if he'd take her hint. After all, sooner or later she'd have to tell him who she really was.

"Why is that?" Phillip asked.

"Whenever life gets boring you just step into someone else's shoes."

"I suspect it might be more than that," he said thoughtfully. "Some people experiment with different roles because they're trying to find out who they really are."

She laughed, gave her head a shake and sipped her tea. Then she stared at him long and hard. "You think so?"

"Could be in your case. Maybe being a horse trainer isn't what you'd most like to be."

"But I love horses," she objected, clinging to her role out of sheer stubbornness.

"And you were doing great with Eros. But that doesn't

mean your heart doesn't yearn for something more than coddling wealthy folks' pets.'' She pouted at him, and he wished he could figure out what she was thinking at that moment. He suspected she was more than a little embarrassed by having taken the fall. ''Never mind. Eros is a troubled spirit. If he hadn't wanted you on him, he would have lost you long before that jump, despite all your experience.''

She considered that for a moment and felt a happy little thrill inside of her. She had done well, hadn't she? Alex put down her teacup. ''Do you know what I want more than anything?''

''A blueberry scone instead of the raisin?''

She waved him off. ''No, silly. I mean, what I really, really want in life.''

''Oh, now we're into the heavy stuff.'' He shook his head, mocking her, and sat back down on the edge of her chaise to listen.

''I'm serious.'' She straightened up, seized his hand and brought it into her lap. At once, he was conscious of the warmth of her flesh beneath the thin robe. ''I want to be someone who makes a difference. I want to do something special and important with my life.''

''I'd say you have every opportunity to do that,'' he commented. ''Just choose. There are plenty of charities out there.''

''No!'' she shouted, startling him with the emotion and strength in her voice. ''That's just it. I don't want to chair committees or sponsor fund-raisers like rich women. I want to *do* things, not oversee others as they do them.''

He nodded. The urge was all too familiar. Hadn't he felt restless, hemmed in by his estate and people's expectations of him? He didn't have to work to keep a roof over his head. He could travel anywhere he pleased. Yet he felt discontent.

"Do you know where Silverdorn is?" he asked her suddenly.

"You mean, your kingdom, Prince?" She shook her head.

"It no longer exists. At one time it was a small region on the border between France and Italy, a much-contested territory. My family lost it to other monarchs centuries ago, but we have retained our titles as tradition allows."

She giggled.

"What's so funny?" he demanded, offended that his family's plight seemed humorous to her.

"You're...*homeless?*"

He smiled slowly. "Not homeless...but country-less, yes. That does sound ridiculous, doesn't it? Someone with as much wealth and property to be without a country."

She was laughing harder now. "The homeless prince. Oh, oh God— Ouch!"

"Hurts, huh? Serves you right for making fun of the less fortunate," he teased.

She cradled her aching shoulder with her good arm. "Cut it out. You'll make me laugh harder."

Tears formed in her pretty eyes, and Phillip perversely felt like doing something to make them shine even more. He reached out, making tickling motions with his fingers as he neared her stomach, and her eyes widened in panic.

"Don't you dare! No fair torturing the wounded."

"I think you're far less wounded than you pretend," he accused. "In fact, you're so used to acting out roles, you probably don't know *who* you really are."

The look on her face stunned him to silence. Her laughter immediately ceased. Pushing herself up off the chaise with a flinch of pain, she walked away from him down the terrace steps toward the water.

"Alex, what did I say?" he called after her. "I didn't mean to hurt your feelings."

She tugged her robe closer around her body and moved stiffly down the steps as he chased after her. "Just leave me alone."

"No. Obviously I've hit on a sore spot. I'm sorry. I really am. Tell me why what I said offended you."

She shook her head and kept on walking. He caught up to her with no trouble, as she was slowed down by her shoulder.

"Alex?" He stepped in front of her. There were tears again, but not happy ones. Her face was contorted in a secret agony. He carefully enfolded her in his arms, taking care not to put pressure on her injured shoulder. "Tell me. I don't want to make the same mistake again."

She drew a shuddering breath and rested her cheek against his chest. "You're right," she whispered. "I don't know who I am. Not really."

"But that was just a joke. You're an excellent trainer, I'm sure. You just had a bad day. Besides, you're too intelligent a woman not to know who you are."

She looked up at him, green fire in her eyes. "Do *you*, Phillip? Do you know who you are?"

"I'm not sure what you mean." He was suddenly aware of the heat of her body, of the luscious curves, hollows and soft swells that were her breasts and hips. She was tucked into his body, and the scant clothing she wore seemed inconsequential protection. He was aroused.

Rotten timing, Kinrowan, he thought ruefully.

"You are a prince by title, without a kingdom. How else would you define yourself?" she demanded.

He didn't know. "Well, I'm a man who loves horses

and competes by jumping them. And I've always been fascinated by sailing and I have several boats."

"I'm not talking about things you *own*," she said sharply. "I'm talking about who you are, deep in your soul."

He was at a loss. What was she talking about?

She pulled away from him to pace the path between the grand house and the intoxicatingly blue ocean. "All right. I'll give you an example. Say there's this young woman who has been raised in a wealthy family. All of her life, she's had everything she ever wanted. Money was no object. All of her friends were rich, too. Because that's the way people are. They group themselves by financial status, always wanting to be with their own kind, never wanting to associate with anyone with less in their bank accounts or who go to less prestigious schools."

He wasn't sure who she was talking about, but he didn't interrupt her to ask.

"And this young woman wants more than anything to be special, not because of her father's money, but because of something she herself can do or be. Something that's her very own and from her heart. Only she can't be special because she doesn't know what that something is." Her voice was so tight, he feared it might snap like a fragile crystal goblet.

She blinked up at him. "Or maybe she's just someone who works in stables, but she still wants to be special. Then she thinks she finds it when she falls in love. And she begins to believe that she will be happy with the man she's chosen, and they will have children together and live as anyone else in love does, regardless of how much or how little money they have. Because their love will transport them above the crudeness of the financial and social worlds they've been stuck in all of their lives.'' She went dead silent, so suddenly it took him by surprise.

"That's a lovely dream," he said quietly, not knowing what else to say. That last bit, he realized, she'd been talking about herself. "And does she find happiness with her true love?"

"She does, for a while. In fact, she follows the dream perfectly—choosing her bridesmaids, selecting a beautiful gown, ordering the cake and designing a lovely summer wedding on the lakeside. She is in heaven, or so she thinks, and then…'' Her voice trailed off and tears flowed down her cheeks. Phillip ached to hold her again, but he sensed she wouldn't allow him to comfort her.

"And then," he guessed, "the creep did something unspeakably horrible to spoil her dream."

"The creep did indeed." She angrily dashed the tears away with the heel of her hand. "I—*she* heard him talking to her maid of honor. Flirting. Bragging, really. He'd had too much to drink after the rehearsal party and he told the bride's best friend that he was, in effect, marrying her for her—for her connection with the Connellys."

"I see." He felt her pain as his own. The story was too close to his experience with marriage. He didn't want to hear the rest, but there was no stopping Alex. She dropped the pretense of disguising the bride as if she were someone other than herself.

"Of course, when I confronted him, he just laughed off my anger. He claimed he was just trying to shock Jessy. It was all a game, or so he said."

"But you knew it was true," he put in.

"Yes, it was all very clear suddenly. There were things he'd said and done while we were dating that I'd chosen to ignore or forgive. Suddenly they all made sense. He had even gone so far as to put off our honeymoon so that he could complete a project he was working on for Grant Connelly.''

''I can't imagine any man not wanting to honeymoon with you, Alex,'' he murmured, then bit his lip. Where had that come from?

She didn't seem to have heard him. ''There were other things. *I knew* he'd been using me, and I could see our future. I'd be just like so many of my girlfriends who married for what they thought was love, only to find they were assets. I couldn't bear to be used that way.''

''So you walked out on him.''

''Yes. I did.'' She looked down at her folded hands, her eyes dry now. ''That phone message from several days ago. It was from him. From Robert.''

He could feel how difficult it was for her to even mention his name. ''He wants to reconcile?''

She nodded. ''Predictable. He's not one to give up easily.''

''How has your family taken all of this?''

She shrugged. ''They want me to be happy. The thing is, I haven't told them yet what my reasons were for walking out on the wedding. When and if I do, I know they'll support my decision.''

Phillip reached out, touched her arm, and she didn't draw away. ''We have a lot in common.''

She looked at him sideways then let a strained smile lift her lips. ''You left your bride at the altar?''

''Would that had been the case,'' he said bitterly. ''Come.'' He took her hand. ''Let's walk.''

He led her down the stone path to the beach, white sand and shells. She was barefoot. He kicked off his sandals and they walked in the water's edge until he found the words he'd never spoken to another person. They seemed necessary now, since she'd shared so much of herself with him.

"My wife was a very beautiful woman. She was the sort of woman who walked into a room and every male head turned. Blond, a figure like a goddess, a taste for clothes that was flawless. She was clever and flattering and knew how to please a man."

She was listening intently to him as he continued.

"I was beyond proud when she agreed to marry me. I believed we would make the most amazing couple. Forever. You see, I'm a traditionalist at heart. I believe marriage should happen once in a lifetime, if it's done right. And that's the only way I wanted to do it—right."

Alex stopped walking and faced him, her eyes bright. "Yes. That's how it should be. So what spoiled it for you?"

"Almost a year after our wedding, I suggested we start planning a family. She didn't say no, but she put off further discussion, making excuses. Then, when I suggested we take a month-long cruise, just the two of us since we had so little time together because of our social obligations, she said she couldn't do it."

"Why?"

"I don't remember. There were so many excuses that involved her hobbies, her clubs, her friends. I realized that the real problem was we'd never been alone together for more than a few hours at a time. There was always a party or a Grand Prix or an invitation from friends. We'd never really gotten to know each other."

"But that was the way she liked it," Alex whispered.

He was amazed by her insight. "Yes, I'm convinced of that now. She liked sex well enough, but she didn't want the true intimacy of marriage—the melding of souls. She liked the lifestyle, having unlimited money to spend, always having a party or a tea to rush off to."

"It was what she was used to."

"No." He shook his head. "She hadn't come from money. In fact, I later did some investigating and found out she had been a secretary to a CEO of an international firm. There'd been a scandal when his wife discovered their affair, and Tanya had been dismissed, but not without a beautiful condo on Corsica and a bank account to see her through a year or more. After that she'd been the mistress of a sheik, had an affair with a Texas oilman, and lived with a famous actor twice her age."

"And every time she ended the relationship in better shape than she'd entered it," Alex guessed. "Trading up."

"It seemed. But apparently what she really wanted was marriage and a long-term guarantee of the lifestyle she'd come to love. That's where I came in."

"I'm sorry," Alex murmured. If she had felt betrayed and used, here was a man who had suffered at least as much.

"Believe me," he said as if reading her thoughts, "you're far better off to have learned the truth before the vows."

"She took you for a ton of alimony?"

"More than that. Far, far more." His eyes were incredibly sad. The lines around his mouth were drawn tightly, in defense against an overwhelming wave of emotion that she could see he was struggling against.

Alex looked up at him, feeling a compassion that came from shared tragedy. No one had died, but a part of each of them had perished at the hands of people who had seen their wealth and status as a prize. She knew too well how disappointing it was to learn the person you loved and trusted with your future cared nothing for you, only for what you owned and could give them.

Impulsively, she raised up on tiptoe and kissed Phillip lightly on the cheek. "Will we survive?" she whispered.

"I suppose so." He looked down at her, and in that moment his expression changed from one of recalled pain to interest. Interest of the male-female variety.

"Oh, no," she murmured shaking her head and starting to pull away from him. His arms closed around her, bringing her back to him.

"Why not?" he asked, a twinkle in his eyes that let her know he was healing perhaps faster than she. "In many ways we're perfect for each other. Neither of us cares a whit about money. And social climbing? You don't seem the type. Unless—" he glared at her in mock concern "—unless you're after my title."

"Like I care," she snorted in a very unladylike way.

"See?"

She wriggled in his arms but didn't dare exert too much force with her shoulder still being so tender. "There's the issue of physical attraction," she pointed out. "I don't make a habit of sleeping with just anyone. There has to be that spark, that something special. It doesn't happen very often."

"True," he admitted. He made a show of looking her up and down as much as their close position allowed. "You're not really my type, after all."

"And I don't need another man in my life after Robert. I'd be just as happy to stay on my own for the next decade or so."

"You're not attracted to me at all, are you?" he asked casually.

"Not a bit," she lied.

"Just what I thought." But his eyes twinkled, and she

doubted he believed her. "So, in effect, we'd be safe together. I mean, for the purposes of social engagements."

She frowned. "I don't understand."

"If people assumed we were a couple, I wouldn't be stalked by other women who were out to take me for my money or title. And you'd have companionship without having to worry about a commitment you don't want."

She thought about that for a moment. "I guess you're right. It would be nice to have someone to be with, without getting all worked up about whether or not he loves me, or if he will or won't be around a month from now."

"You see? It's a liberating idea, isn't it? And since you enjoy acting out other people's lives, I'm sure you could pull off the role of the spoiled deb for my mother. I'll even help you work on your dramatic skills."

"So you aren't turned on by holding me this way?" she asked, still just a little suspicious. After all, she knew she wasn't unattractive. And her ego did rebel just a little at the thought that he might not feel anything for her.

"Turned on? No way. Might as well be hugging my sister."

She nodded. "In that case, let's make a pact. We'll be lovers, in the eyes of the world."

"In the eyes of the world," he repeated as solemnly as if he were swearing on his life. But there was a glimmer in his amber eyes that didn't seem to match his tone. "We need to seal our pact. Do you think a kiss would be appropriate?"

"A businesslike kiss just to show neither of us has a chance of falling for the other, right?"

"Absolutely."

They were already as close as two bodies could be. All he had to do was lean down a few inches. She smelled the sweetness of his breath as his lips moved over hers. They touched briefly, dryly, perfunctorily.

"All right?" she asked.

He scowled down at her. "That wouldn't convince anyone I was hot for you."

"A problem," she agreed. "Let's try again."

Even though the first kiss hadn't even approached passionate, Alex had felt something. It wasn't a sensation she'd experienced before, with Robert or any other man. It was something between a tickle and a twinge down low in her body. It was a feeling she liked…and wanted more of.

This time she rose up to meet Phillip halfway, and she opened her mouth as she would if the man she was kissing were a man she was in love with. She assumed the role, and he took her lead. His tongue flicked over her teeth and darted between her lips as he tasted her. She let her head fall back as she savored his kiss. As his hand came up behind her head to support her, he pressed harder, their kiss deepening. She felt a chill, then a blaze, then a mysterious and delicious warmth through every part of her body.

Yes, this was a kiss that would convince anyone they were lovers.

This was a kiss that might even convince *her* that Phillip, prince of Silverdorn, actually felt something for her. Even though he swore he didn't.

At last their lips slowly parted. They both were breathing heavily.

"Well," she said, her eyelashes fluttering, her pulse too fast, her flesh tingling as he released her, "that should do the trick, don't you think?"

Phillip cleared his throat and smiled weakly. "I suspect

so.'' He looked away from her, then took a deep breath. ''It will be an effort, though. This acting stuff takes a lot out of a person.''

More than you'll ever know, she thought.

Three

The days passed, and Phillip cancelled both social and business engagements to remain at the estate. He didn't miss his old routine, and he didn't miss competing at the Paris Grand Prix, for which he'd been preparing over the past three weeks. The focus of his life seemed to have shifted without his noticing, but that was all right with him. He spent hours with Alex, sometimes just talking with her or sharing a meal, more often reading quietly in the same room with her. She had discovered his library and selected from it several first-edition novels she had read years before and loved.

"Books are true friends that stay with you through your whole life," she said sleepily one night. "They don't criticize you. They're never too busy to spend time with you, and when you're reading—" she stretched and yawned, as contented as a cat "—you can transform yourself into anyone in the world."

One day while she was in his library, she came across three long rolls of paper. Thinking they might be maps of Altaria, she unrolled one and found it to be a diagram of a boat, incomplete but beautifully and carefully drawn. The others were also sketches of watercraft in various stages. She suspected Phillip had paid someone to custom design a yacht for him. Why not? He could afford just about any luxury he wished. She rolled up the sketches and stuck them back behind the books where she'd found them, giving them no further thought.

As soon as Alex felt able to sit a horse, she asked Phillip to take her down to the stables and let her ride inside one of the rings. He was concerned about her reinjuring her shoulder but she waved off his objections.

"I won't try to ride Eros, but if you have a horse that's a little more dependable, I could use some exercise. I don't want to get rusty," she added, sticking to her horse trainer's image.

"I know just the horse for the recuperating wounded," he said with a wink that set her smiling.

He had arranged for her clothing to be brought from the castle days earlier, so she had her own riding clothes to change into that morning after their Continental breakfast of warm rolls, jam and coffee. Her arm was still in a sling, but she was insistent she could manage the reins with one hand.

Phillip phoned the stables to have Maxmillian saddled for her. "Max is an old trouper of the Grand Prix circuit. He's like riding a pillow."

She laughed. "I don't think I've ever heard that expression."

He grinned. "You'll see."

Max was a gorgeous, wide-hipped, sixteen-hand-high Thoroughbred with chestnut coloring and golden eyes. He observed her calmly from beneath a black forelock. She patted him on the side of his thick neck, and said, "Let's be friends, old man."

He seemed to listen to her and understand. She mounted him, and Phillip was right. He felt like a big, overstuffed sofa on hooves, broad and softly muscled between her thighs, moving at an effortless and smooth gait. She barely felt any rise and fall in his canter. His gallop was flat and easy, like silk drawn through the Mediterranean air.

Phillip had said he no longer jumped the horse competitively, but the animal was capable. She didn't want to force Max beyond his limits, but when she turned him toward a low rail, the gelding took it easily and seemed happy to do more. She cleared two feet with him, then a three-foot wall, but stopped at that because her shoulder was starting to hurt.

When she brought Max around to the gate and stopped, Phillip was watching her appreciatively. "You look great up there." His eyes were intense, reminding her of their shared kisses. Kisses she had thought about far too often in the past days.

"He'd make anyone look wonderful," she said with a sigh, leaning down to hug the horse's gleaming neck. "We should arrange for him to give Eros lessons."

Phillip chuckled. "Now there's a thought. One horse to another. Leave humans out of the picture entirely." His gaze shifted, and she followed it to the water's edge, below the long expanse of manicured lawn.

A flock of sailboats skimmed the azure water. Phillip's gaze grew distant, dreamy.

"What is it?" she asked.

"It's been ages since I took time off to sail."

"You have boats. Why not go for a sail?"

"I do have boats," he said. "But not the one I want."

"So buy it," she said simply.

His wistful smile caressed the distant water. "It doesn't exist."

Alex lifted a leg over Max's head and slid off to the ground. The landing jolted her shoulder and she winced.

"I don't understand," she said, coming around to face him.

Placing a hand on her good shoulder, he looked over her head. "It's something I've dreamt of since I was a boy. A boat anyone could sail, and most anyone could afford. Nothing fancy, but perfect in design, seaworthy and large enough for a couple with their children."

She had never seen such an expression of pure love and longing in another person's eyes. It must be wonderful, she thought, to be the object of those emotions. But Phillip wasn't in love with a woman, he was in love with a boat. A fantasy boat.

"Tell me more about it," she prompted.

He opened his mouth as if to answer her then slowly shook his head and the remoteness dropped away from his eyes. "It's nothing. One of those things you invent in your head as a child and have to let go once the realities of adulthood hit you."

"Phillip—"

He looked down at her, his expression suddenly blank. It was as if he'd completely forgotten their previous conversation. "So, what do you suggest I do now about Eros? Give up on him as a competitive jumper? I wish you could have seen him. He was magnificent."

Alex sighed in frustration but let him change the subject for the moment. "Don't count him out yet. I still think if you take his retraining slowly enough, he may come around."

"But who's going to train him? You said that using my regular trainer wouldn't be a good idea."

She shrugged. "*I'd* like to try riding Eros again."

His expression darkened. "Perhaps on the flat, but I don't know about—"

"Listen, there's something else you probably haven't considered," she interrupted with a new thought. "Maybe Eros was never meant to be a jumper." She started leading the chestnut back toward the stables. "Just because he was trained to jump doesn't mean it's in his soul. Maybe he knows that better than anyone."

Phillip considered this new idea. "We're trained to do a lot of things, aren't we? You and I and everyone else. I mean, from the time we're born there are expectations, roles, right and wrong things to do and say. It's all pounded into us."

She frowned and handed Max's reins to the stable boy, who walked the big creature into the stable. She looked up into the sun, almost at its zenith, but had to blink and turn her eyes away from the hot, orange sphere. "I suppose. Like, my parents have always had certain expectations about the kind of person I should be. They'd never, ever tell me I'd disappointed them. But sometimes I worry that I won't be good enough for them...you know, be worthy of their love." She swallowed and her throat felt suddenly dry and raw.

Phillip touched her arm and gazed at her with compassion.

"And my friends—I don't dare guess what they think of me. Flighty Alexandra, she never knows what she wants or sticks to anything for long."

Phillip's arm came around her and, without thinking about it, she leaned into the curve of his strong body. "Poor misunderstood Alex," he breathed.

"I guess I don't make it easy on them," she admitted. "One minute I'm sure I'm going to be the perfect wife and mother, just be happy with my little family. The next, I'm hot to take skydiving lessons. It's always been that way with me."

She looked up at Phillip and was surprised by how intently he was listening to her. I could get lost in those eyes, she thought to herself with a shiver that wasn't entirely unpleasant. I could sink into them like slipping into a warm bath and stay forever. "One summer I decided I wanted to be a dancer on Broadway."

"Before you got involved with horses?"

"Yes," she said, avoiding his too perceptive gaze. "Before then. I moved to New York and actually had the nerve to audition for the chorus in three different musicals."

"You're kidding!" He laughed, but she didn't feel he was making fun of her; he was just surprised by the idea. "Had you taken dance lessons?"

"When I was a little girl, sure. But not for ages, and not at the level of the other dancers who were trying out with me."

"Did you get a part?"

She snorted. "Not even close. They were polite—don't-call-us, we'll-call-you sort of thing. I didn't go back to the theaters for the final word. By then I'd changed my mind and wanted to be a writer, a novelist."

"With your imagination, you'd probably do great," he said encouragingly.

"You think so?" She pondered that one. "Well, I didn't give that career much of a go, either. I spent three months holed up in a moldy, Greenwich Village flat I shared with three other girls. I wrote all day and partied all night, at first. Then I wrote just in the mornings and the parties started earlier. In the end I wrote for an hour a day if I was lucky. That's when I decided to be a librarian.''

"A librarian?" His eyes sparkled with amusement, as if he wasn't sure how much of her story was true and how much she was inventing to entertain him.

She nodded. "The scholarly type, with horn-rimmed spectacles, hair pulled into a bun, whispery voice. But I found out you needed a degree for that, and I didn't want to go to school anymore, so that was that.''

"My little chameleon," he murmured.

She was shocked not by his comparison, but by his use of the pronoun. *My.* She wondered if he'd even heard his own words.

After a moment he continued. "I have a proposition for you," he said.

"Oh?"

"We've already agreed in theory to help each other out. As long as you're available in this part of the world, you will be my significant other. In return, I'll fend off Robert if he shows up, since I'm your new love interest and will be the very jealous type." A sexy sparkle lit his eyes that made her suspicious of his motives, but he continued too quickly to allow her time to figure it out. "As part of your job, you can start by helping me out of a tight spot with my mother."

"Your mother," she repeated. "How's that?"

He walked her back toward the main house. "She wants me to meet the daughter of an old school friend of hers. Apparently the young woman is spending a few weeks with Mother at her villa here on the island. I'm supposed to come for dinner sometime this week. You can accompany me and bring along your obviously active imagination."

Alex grinned. "Let's see, I could be a princess from

Eastern Europe, or even better, a dancer you met at a top-less bar!'' She laughed at the prospect.

"That might be overdoing it," he cautioned. "How about just being—" He broke off and frowned at her. "My God, I don't even know your last name!"

"Anderson." It was the first one that came to mind.

Alex looked up at Phillip, having half a mind to end her game and come clean right then and there. But if Phillip knew she was one of the heiresses he so despised, she sensed he'd no longer find her such good company. And she really was having a lot of fun with him.

"Will you do it, Alex?" he asked eagerly.

She ran her tongue between her lips and looked up at him. Their eyes met and, for an instant, she was convinced she would have done anything he asked. Anything at all. "I'll try. Sure. Why not?" She aimed for a casual tone, then added impulsively, "If you'll do something for me in return."

"What's that?"

She wasn't really sure what she had in mind, but it seemed important that she strike a deal now. Who knew when she might need a favor? "I'll let you know as soon as I figure it out," she said hastily. "Now, when is this dinner?"

The night of Genevieve Kinrowan's dinner party, Alex removed the muslin sling the doctor had given her. The joint felt only a little stiff when she tried to move it, but the ugly thing didn't advance the image she had imagined for Phillip's lover. And that was who she would be that night, his new mistress, at least as far as his mother and her guests were concerned.

She wore a white gauze dress that came up in a halter and looped around her neck before dipping low between her breasts. To give herself an airy summertime look, she chose a silver jewelry set with turquoise that she'd bought in Arizona on a trip with friends. Her black hair was moussed into a short, sophisticated style that bared her long neck.

When she glided down the stairs of Phillip's house into the foyer, he looked up at her, and for a moment there was astonishment and something more in his eyes. "You look unbelievable," he said and held a hand out to guide her down the last two steps.

"Is that good or bad, as far as your mother is concerned?" she asked.

"Very good, as far as I'm concerned, too." He threaded her hand through the crook of his arm.

He wore a tuxedo that had been tailored for him. She admired the workmanship and wondered if it was Italian or English—the cut was unusual with broader shoulders and a slimmer waist than most, but then it might have been cut that way to fit his muscular physique.

A midnight-blue Mazarati was parked out front and that was what they drove to his mother's villa on the far side of the island. He had put the top down, and the wind ruffled Alex's loosely tousled hair. In a playful mood, she was prepared to put on her best act. She imagined little things she might do to show she and Phillip were involved—a brush of her fingertips along his lapel as she flicked off imaginary lint, a sideways glance and half smile that carried private meanings, positioning herself close enough to him in a circle of conversation so that her hip occasionally bumped up against his. She smiled to herself. A new role, and one she could really throw herself into with gusto. Fantastic!

The villa wasn't small or quaint or modest as some of the pastel stucco homes on the island that they'd passed.

It was modern, glassy, perched arrogantly on a cliff over-looking a breathtakingly blue harbor as if it owned the scene spread before it. She immediately felt uncomfortable there, the way she felt with the people she'd called her friends all through her school days when she'd visited their lavish homes. She was used to expensive surroundings, but her parents' home had always had a comfortable, lived-in feeling about it, with children's toys strewn around and cozy nooks you could cuddle up in with a book. Here, like other homes built for the pure purpose of impressing guests or outdoing your neighbors, she felt on edge. All the more reason to become someone other than Grant Connelly's daughter from Chicago.

Phillip left the Mazarati in the drive and a valet drove it off to a spot on the lawn with a few dozen others. They walked through high wooden portals that were the front entrance to the house, past statues that could only have been classic Greek, not revival, and into a formal parlor crowded with guests in expensive clothes and far too much jewelry. It was a crowd Alex was familiar with but had never liked. She straightened, aware of the dull ache in her shoulder and regretted having removed the sling, then let her eyes drift half-closed in a bored attitude meant to be-little the glitz in the room.

"Mother, I knew we'd find you in the middle of every-thing," Phillip called out, dropping a kiss on the cheek of an elegant, too thin woman in her fifties. "I'm sorry we are a little late. Something came up at the last minute."

Alex put on a standard pleased-to-meet-you smile for Genevieve Kinrowan Courvoisier. Phillip had explained that her fourth husband was French, but he lived most of the year in his own country, tending his vineyards, while she preferred Altaria for its climate and social life. It didn't seem worth marrying, Alex thought, living apart that way.

If she ever again considered marriage, which she seriously doubted, it would be an all-the-way proposition. No long-distance living arrangements. No social or financial matches for practical purposes. It would only be for love.

"And you must be the young woman my Phillip told me about over the telephone," Genevieve said, studying her coyly. "To be honest, I wasn't sure you existed. He's fond of coming up with excuses for not attending my parties."

"I can't see why he would," Alex said in a honeyed voice. "You have a beautiful home, and I'm sure your choice of company is just as interesting."

Genevieve's smile became a notch more genuine. "Why, thank you, my dear." Her glance shifted hastily to a young woman in a red dress who was working her way across the room toward them. There was a subtle warning in Genevieve's expression, as if she didn't want the woman to approach now, but the blonde kept coming with a wide-eyed expression, her sights set on Phillip.

"Oh, hello!" she said to Phillip's back, then tapped him on the shoulder to make him turn around. "Your mother said you'd be here and…well, I wasn't going to come but then she insisted that I meet you. I'm glad I did." She held out the back of her hand as if she expected him to kiss it.

Genevieve looked in pain. Alex nearly giggled. Phillip hesitated but then accepted her hand and lowered it into a conventional handshake.

"Pleased to meet you," he said. "And you are?"

"Patricia Rutledge. I'm visiting from London, but actually I'm an American. Daddy is in oil."

"He must be very sticky, then," Alex whispered, covering her comment with a demure smile.

Only Phillip caught her words. He tensed at her side, but said nothing.

"And you are?" Patricia asked, looking at Alex as if she hadn't noticed her before that very moment.

Phillip made the final introductions.

"Your family is from Texas, then?" Alex asked. "The oil," she added by way of explanation.

"Oh, no. Oklahoma," chirped Patricia, wrinkling her nose. "Kinda dusty. It's much prettier here this time of year. All this blue sky and water and— Oh, my, what a lot of pretty things Lady Courvoisier has." Patricia moved closer to Phillip and gazed up at him with unmasked interest. "You're almost as tall as my brothers. I didn't think European men grew all that big."

"They can grow quite large," Alex said innocently. She lifted a hand and stroked her fingertips down the back of Phillip's neck in a playful gesture. "When they're—"

Phillip coughed into his hand, interrupting disaster. "Have you seen much of Altaria, Patricia?" he asked.

Alex played with the short hairs at the back of his neck. Patricia's eyes followed the movement of her fingertips with belated comprehension. He outlined sights she should see on her visit, while Alex casually started her own conversation with his mother.

An hour later, they were driving away from the party, laughing conspiratorially at the show they'd put on. Genevieve had been totally convinced they were a couple. Phillip congratulated Alex on her performance. "You read my mother's tastes perfectly. Right up to her favorite jewelers and designers in Rome."

"I've been around people like her all of my life. By now it almost comes naturally."

He slanted a look at her she couldn't quite interpret.

"What?" she asked.

"Nothing."

"There *is* something. You were thinking about what

happened at the party, something about me. Say it.'' Her voice had taken on a defensive edge, even though he had said nothing negative about her.

His eyes shadowed, he bit the words off. ''It seemed far too easy for you.''

''What was easy?''

''Lying.''

''I don't *lie!*'' She was appalled. After all, what she did was more like…storytelling.

Phillip shrugged as if it was a forgone conclusion. ''Pretending to be a pampered rich woman is a form of a lie for someone who spends her days in stalls with sweaty horses.''

''You *asked* me to put on a show for your mother, and I did. She bought it. You should be pleased.''

''I'm relieved that she'll leave me alone and won't be foisting off debutantes on me for a while. But I'm worried about you,'' he said tightly.

''Well, don't waste the effort,'' she snapped. ''I can take care of myself.'' She scowled at him. ''Why should you worry about me, anyway?''

He stared out the windshield as he drove, his attention seemingly fixed on the road. But she sensed he was struggling to find the right words. ''I know who you are, Alex.''

''You do?'' Her cheeks felt suddenly flushed. How had he figured out she was a Connelly?

''You're just a simple girl who's spent too much time around the rich.'' He pulled over to the side of the road and turned in the driver's seat to face her. ''I was right the first time—you really don't know who you are, do you?''

She snorted at him. ''Give me a break.''

''It's true, you've pretended to be other people for so long you've lost sight of who Alex Anderson is. Or maybe you never gave yourself time to learn in the first place.''

She huffed at him and rolled her eyes. "That's ridiculous. Of course I know who I am!"

"Do you? Back there at the party, you slipped into the role of my society lover without batting an eye. By the time we left, my mother was convinced you were her clone."

"So? I just did what you told me to do."

"No. It's one thing being a good actress. It's another when you can't find your way home again, when you leap from one role to another, never finding the real you to come back to."

Tears welled in her eyes and she fought them back. She flung open the car door and staggered away from the sleek silhouette onto the sandy beach. The wind tugged at her hair, but it remained in its moussed coif. She faced into the wind and drew in huge gulps of salty air.

He was too close to the truth and it hurt. But the pretending had seemed innocent enough at the time. Only for the fun of it had she played at being someone of whom his mother would approve. To break up the boredom, to amuse herself. All of her friends thought she was a hoot. They loved being around her, even if Phillip, prince of Silver-what's-it didn't appreciate her!

"Alex."

He had left the car and, suddenly, was beside her. But she refused to turn and look at him.

"I didn't mean to hurt your feelings. But you admitted to me that you want to find yourself."

"I meant career-wise." She sniffled. "I meant, as in choosing something to do that's important and special. Something more important than what I do now. That's different from not knowing who you are."

"Maybe. Maybe not." His voice was low and patient,

waiting for her to gather up her emotions, untangle the knot of her feelings.

"I just want to learn how to live my life in a way that makes me happy," she said, the words trembling across her lips. That was the absolute truth. She wanted to feel good about herself. And she supposed that using a God-given talent for the benefit of others might have something to do with that. But did she have such a talent?

"You're not sure what makes you happy, is that it?"

She dipped her chin in a half nod. Her eyes were locked on the horizon—the division between sky and sea, between the untouchable atmosphere and the liquid from which all life came.

"Maybe you should investigate alternate lifestyles," he suggested, "rather than mimicking different people. Give yourself a chance to see what's important to you, what you really like."

"I don't understand what you mean." At last, she forced herself to face him.

"Well, we could start simple, from the beginning."

"Like with Eros?" A tiny, tentative smile lifted one corner of her lips.

"Yes. Like with a damaged jumper. Maybe you're not so different. Maybe *I'm* not so different." His hands settled on her shoulders and, with a comforting smile, he pulled her into his chest. She let herself rest against him, and she could feel his heart beating—low, rhythmic, steady, dependable. Soothing. "I have a suggestion," he said at last.

"What's that?" she whispered, not wanting to drown out his life sounds, because she felt she was clinging to them, needing them desperately.

"Let's plan a day—no, a whole weekend. That's even better. We could leave the estate and spend it anywhere we like on the island but not on my estate or at the palace. And we will take only ten American dollars with us to cover everything we need for the two days.''

"Ten dollars?" Alex frowned. She sometimes tossed off a ten-dollar tip to a parking attendant! "That's just loose change. No one can *live* on that." The words were out of her mouth before she could stop them. Alex held her breath.

"You told me your parents had to scrape by on almost nothing when you were little," he reminded her. "Now you're afraid you can't do it?"

"Of course I'm not afraid. I just don't understand why—"

"People get by on very little every day. Ordinary people who live full, happy lives but aren't rich. Ten dollars pocket money for the weekend. I say we can make it." His tawny eyes flashed in challenge. Was he mocking her or really trying to help?

"This is a bet, then?" she asked.

"No money involved. I'm offering you a chance to prove yourself. Use that imagination of yours."

She decided she didn't mind the way his eyes sparked, daring her. But there was something more, something stronger passing between them. It was electric and sensual, and it curled restlessly inside of her. She tried to push the distracting sensation aside.

"All right," she said to him. "I'm game."

"Good." He moved closer, bringing his head down to gaze into her eyes, and now...*now* she was certain he was going to kiss her.

What would she do if he did? A lump closed off her throat, and her palms felt damp and hot at the same time.

"Do we get to take the Mazarati for the weekend?" she

asked, hastily turning away from him and toward the car, her heart beating an erratic tattoo.

"No. The gas alone would break us."

She nodded and kept on moving. "Then we walk everywhere?"

He caught up with her, and she was sure he was grinning at her, but she didn't dare turn to look. "Not everywhere. I have one idea for transportation that won't cost us anything."

"And that is?"

"You'll see," he said, stopping at the car to hold the door open for her. "In the morning."

Four

As attire for her weekend adventure Alex chose an airy peasant-style dress with a full skirt, good walking sandals and a pretty shawl. She imagined herself as a gypsy, roaming the countryside between quaint villages. Telling a fortune. Pinching a few coins from an innocent tourist. Undulating her hips to the sensuous strains of a flamenco guitar played before a fire in a forest clearing. Very, very romantic.

She met Phillip on the patio of his villa. He handed her a rose. "For my lady. And it didn't cost a penny as it was picked from the prince's garden when he wasn't looking."

She laughed at him and breathed deeply of the bloom's heady fragrance. Why did everything appear brighter, smell fresher, feel more alive here in Altaria than back home in Chicago? In this exotic world, she felt like a new person. Her heartbreak had been left behind in the asphalt streets.

Alex looked up at Phillip. "It's lovely. Thank you."

Phillip smiled, thinking how other women he'd known, his wife for one, would have tossed off his gift of a single bloom as a silly gesture. They'd expect nothing less than two dozen pricey hothouse roses. Coming from such an unsophisticated upbringing, Alex was refreshingly different. Not spoiled, not demanding. She seemed surprised and pleased with the least gesture. How delightful!

He checked out her outfit. "A dress? We may be walking a fair amount these two days."

She shrugged. "I'll be fine." After all, gypsy women didn't wear trendy Capri pants or blue jeans. She needed the appropriate props, right?

"If you're sure," he said doubtfully. "Are you ready?"

"Absolutely!"

Her heart leapt at the challenge presented by the next two days. Imagine, making do on just ten dollars and their own wits. What a lark it would be! She couldn't wait to tell her girlfriends back home.

That is, if they were still speaking to her after she'd called off the wedding. There had been the not-so-little matter of thousands of dollars having been spent on bridesmaids' gowns, shoes dyed to match, coordinating jewelry, appointments at the spa for hair, massages, manicures—all for nothing.

Alex flinched at the memory of the inconvenience she'd caused so many people. What if she was wrong? What if she had thrown away her future?

No, she thought fiercely, she knew what she'd heard and she had Justin's observations to back her up. Robert had brought their disastrous breakup on himself. *He* was the one who should be blamed, not her. She shook off stinging memories, determined to leave the past behind.

"Do we have breakfast here first or on our way?" she asked excitedly.

Phillip gave her an amused sideways glance. "A meal served by Cook would cost well over our allowance for the whole weekend."

"Oh, so we're starting right now, this very minute?"

"Yes." He took her hand and began walking down the drive. She matched his stride with enthusiasm, humming as she threw her head back and let the morning sun warm her face. They passed the stables, then a low cedar-shingled boathouse and a pale golden sand beach, still part of Phillip's property.

She was already hungry. "Is there a place in town we can get something to eat? I mean, just to take the edge off my grumbly tummy so I can concentrate better on walking?"

He laughed at her, delighted that she was playing along so well. With her plebian background she would be much more familiar with missed meals and spending thriftily than he would. "You sound like Pooh Bear. Grumbly in your tummy—isn't that what the A. A. Milne books said?"

As a small boy he had been read them by his British nanny, which was one reason his English was so good. He'd grown up speaking equal parts of the island patois, Italian and English. Later, he'd attended private schools in the United States, and he'd lost his British accent. But he still recalled the charming Milne characters with fondness.

One day, perhaps, there would be a little boy in his life. Phillip imagined reading to his own son, and the idea warmed him although the reality of the situation now seemed even further away than he might have imagined a few years ago. The breakup of his marriage had put off any thought of starting a family.

"Rumbly in my tumbly, I think it was," she mused.

"I'm serious, Phillip, we should eat something, don't you think?"

"Oh, we will," he assured her. "The best food a whole American dollar can buy, I'd say."

"*One dollar!* For breakfast for two?" She stopped walking to stare at him. "I'm not a sparrow, you know."

"Whine, whine, whine." He grinned good-naturedly and gave her hand a tug to keep her moving.

They passed a small cove where fishing dories were pulled up onto the sand littered with chalky, sun-bleached cuttlefish bones, pungent seaweed and graceful tangles of driftwood. The scent of brine thickly laced the air, and Alex marveled at the cloudless, blue sky overhead, so rich in color it almost made her believe she could reach out and gather up handfuls of it. Gritty white grains of sand blew across the narrow, unpaved road where they walked, and found secret ways between her toes. The breeze felt cool against her skin, even as the sun warmed her.

Soon she forgot about her hunger and was content to breathe in the fresh air and concentrate on the sensation of her body moving in a pleasant rhythm to Phillip's long, even strides. Down one hill, then up another toward a village that looked as if it had been plucked from a medieval movie set.

Stucco and stone buildings, none taller than two stories, lined narrow streets. They climbed cobbled walkways, passing shops and homes that all looked the same but for a simple wooden plaque to announce the name of an occasional business. At last they came out at the top of the steep hill and into a piazza filled with carts, booths and ragged blankets spread on the ground to display goods.

"It's like a carnival," she remarked as she spun around, taking in all the glorious colors and sounds.

"Weekly *mercato*. Market day," Phillip explained.

"We can take advantage of some good prices here. I thought we'd buy our breakfast, lunch and supper all at once. Later in the day it might be more difficult to find inexpensive food."

"Good idea," she agreed.

They roamed up and down rows of vendors until Phillip found a baker with loaves of crusty bread, small hard rolls the size and weight of cue balls, and rich pastries that smelled like heaven to Alex. Suddenly her hunger reached new and desperate levels.

"Those filled pastries look wonderful," she whispered excitedly in Phillip's ear. "How delicious they'd be with a frothy cup of cappuccino."

"Too expensive. We can buy one of the large loaves of peasant bread, and it will last the day."

He took a moment to bargain with the baker. For less than a dollar in the local currency he purchased a huge loaf of crusty, wheat bread.

"Here, let me have your shawl," he said.

She took it from her shoulders and held it out to him, wondering if he was going to trade it for something like one of the luscious green melons she saw piled high farther down the piazza. Phillip rested the bread in the center of the fabric then tied the ends together to fashion a makeshift shopping bag and slung it over his shoulder.

"First course, done. Now on to the rest."

They purchased fresh oranges, apricots, one very small melon and a generous and fragrant wedge of local cheese from other vendors. "What about something to drink?" Alex asked.

"We'll stick to well water as long as we can find it. Later, we may need to buy a jug of wine to bring with us on the boat."

"Boat? What boat?" She scowled suspiciously at him. "Isn't taking out one of your yachts breaking the rules?"

"Who said anything about a yacht?" His amber eyes crinkled at the corners mischievously.

He must have been a great kid, she thought, and fun to be around. It was a shame people had to grow up. Why not make life a game all the time? Probably that was why she pretended so much—fighting the necessity of growing up. Being an adult could be such a bore. She sighed.

"Something wrong?" Phillip asked.

"No. Just hungry, I guess."

He nodded. "Let's eat down by the water. Less dust and a better view."

Halfway down the hill from town, he found a ledge that overlooked the little harbor of San Pietro. Beyond its aquamarine waters was the darker but no less beautiful Mediterranean Sea. They spread out her shawl and removed all of the food, which looked like a lot until she reminded herself that it was meant to last two people for three meals. But Phillip had done well, spending only a total of four dollars, which left them six for the next day. That is, if they didn't spend any more in the next twenty hours or so.

"Orange or apricot?" he asked.

"Orange," she said, and reached for one of the ruby-skinned fruits. Blood oranges, they were called in the local vernacular. The skin was mottled with crimson splotches. When she peeled it and broke it open, bright orange flesh interspersed with flecks of red dripped with tangy juice and dribbled from her fingertips.

She ate hungrily, while Phillip did the same. He broke off a piece of bread and offered it to her. They consumed their ample meal in silence, and she marveled at how peaceful the world felt.

No traffic noises.

No one telling her how foolish she'd been to walk out on her groom the day before their nuptials.

No urgency to dress and rush off for a luncheon at the club or a day at the office. Not that she knew what a real day in an office would feel like, since she'd never held a real job. There had been several stints of internship at her father's headquarters, but that hadn't seemed to count. Everyone there knew she was Grant Connelly's daughter and went out of their way to *not* make her do any work.

Still, it seemed heavenly to be so far removed from her usual social whirl, to not feel compelled to compete with her friends. There had always been that unspoken rivalry over who wore the most expensive jewelry, who had shopped at the most exclusive stores for their clothes. Malls were passé in her crowd. Nothing short of designer originals from New York, L.A. or European salons would do. Paris was good, Milan was better.

Most of her friends also partied at trendy clubs and bars at least three nights during the week. Flying off to Baja or Vegas for a weekend on the spur of the moment wasn't unusual. If you weren't doing something exciting that cost a small fortune, they'd assume you were sick.

"What are you thinking?" Phillip's deep voice interrupted her less-than-appealing reminiscences of home.

"Nothing much. Just how *different,* how nice it is here."

"It is a beautiful country," he said, "Altaria, Jewel of the Sea—that's what a poet once wrote about it."

"Byron?"

He shook his head. "Could have been Byron, but I can't remember for sure. You enjoy reading, don't you?" He remembered her curled up on the divan in his house, devouring a book from his library.

"I've always loved to read."

"Why didn't the writing work out, then?"

She laughed. "I told you. I didn't have the discipline."

"You're disciplined enough to train horses. I think that takes a lot of concentration and dedication to a difficult job. And you must have worked hard over the years to break into such a male-dominated career. I don't think I've ever met a female trainer before."

An uncomfortable twinge nibbled at her stomach. The lie. It had come back to haunt her again.

She really must confess to him her true identity. But it was such a lovely day, and Alex didn't want to disturb the relaxed camaraderie they had established. After their weekend adventure, she told herself, she would fess up. She was sure he'd share a good laugh with her over her innocent ruse.

"Well, yes, working with horses has been a challenge, of course. But, the other problem with writing is the physical act of sitting in one spot for a long time. I'm not sure I could do that. I have to keep moving."

He shrugged. "You're probably right. You're used to physical work, outdoors. I'm sure that sitting all day at a desk would feel confining."

"Yes," she agreed hastily, "that's exactly how it would be."

Of course, she rarely spent time outdoors, unless you counted skiing in Aspen for a few weeks every year or driving her spunky Fiat convertible with the top down during the summer. But now that she was wandering between quaint villages on Altaria, accompanied by a man who made her heart skip beats every time she looked at him, living without a roof over her head didn't seem bad at all.

She swallowed and took another bite of nectar-dripping orange. "I guess I might go back to writing some day."

"As busy as you are with the horses, I have no doubt you have little time to spend on outside hobbies," he commented and bit off a piece of bread.

"Something like that," she murmured, feeling a sudden tickle of guilt down low in her stomach. She had to change the subject fast or blurt out her admission that she'd tricked him. Now just wasn't the time. "What about you, Phillip? You must have secret dreams. Everyone does."

"Me?" He laughed and shook his head. "What could I want? I have everything."

"Not a family."

He looked at her sharply.

Had she struck a sensitive chord? "I know there's your mother," she clarified. "But I mean, a family of your own. Children. You said you wanted kids."

His expression softened. He tore off another chunk of the bread. "I'd like to have kids some day, but not at the expense of a bad marriage. All the pieces have to fit perfectly. The right mate—her for me, and me for her. I've learned how bad it can be when you make the wrong choice."

That made her feel better about her own dismal situation, although she couldn't let on about that, not yet. "And boats?" she asked. "Where do they fit in?"

"Boats." His eyes glazed over and sought the far horizon. "I like sailing, sure, but...well, the rest of it is a boyhood thing. Something that's no longer possible."

"Tell me about this impossibility of yours."

"Why?" he asked, curious that she should be so insistent about things that no longer mattered.

"I saw the drawings in your library."

He looked blankly at her, at first not understanding. "What drawings?"

"Sketches of boats. Beautiful, sleek craft, but none of

them finished. You hired someone to custom design a sailboat for you, but he never finished?''

He looked away again, his expression thoughtful, the irises of his eyes darkening to a tawny gold. ''I drew those plans.''

''You?''

He nodded. ''A long time ago. As many as ten years, I'd guess.''

She stretched out on the shawl and leaned on one elbow to look up into his face. The breeze off the water kicked up grains of sand and lifted the hem of her skirt, and she noticed his eyes roamed to the long line of her legs. Knowing he was watching her like that made her feel more aware of her body. She decided to ignore the urgent little tugs at her insides, but it wasn't easy.

''Why didn't you finish the drawings?'' she asked.

''Because...I don't know. I suppose it was a combination of distractions. My mother can be a very demanding woman. And there was college, and the many social obligations that go along with—'' He shrugged.

''A title?'' she supplied.

''Yes, and with money of any large amount. I just felt trapped by it all, but couldn't figure out a way to escape.''

''I know exactly what you mean,'' she murmured, feeling very close to him. A second later, she realized with horror that wasn't what a simple working girl would say. Had she given herself away?

Phillip studied her for a long moment. She held her breath.

At last he spoke. ''No, I don't think you ever could understand what it's like, Alex. You didn't come from money, and money exerts powerful pressures of its own. Things are expected of you. You can't just choose what you want to do with your life without getting resistance from family and friends.'' He let out a long, weary breath.

She closed her eyes in relief. ''I see.''

''Then there were practical issues. I didn't have an education in naval design, so I could only take my plans so far before I ran into serious technical problems. Also, I'd have to find a shipbuilder to work with, but I had no idea where to start looking for the right one.''

''So you gave up,'' she stated, saddened at the thought. His one dream. Gone. If she'd had a dream like that, she'd have clung to it till her last breath.

''At the time I didn't think of it as giving up. I simply put the plans aside one day, assuming I'd go back to them.'' He stood up, gathered the orange peels and wrapped the bread in its paper sack. ''Life complicates dreams. I just never picked up where I'd left off.''

They loaded the remaining food into her shawl and he fit his arm through the opening so that their supplies hung in the pouch he'd fashioned over his shoulder. The air was growing warm as the sun rose overhead. They walked down the hill the way they'd come earlier that morning. Alex couldn't stop thinking about all Phillip had shared with her. For some reason, his confidences made her feel special, as if he'd given her a gift, bestowed on her a rare trust. She wanted to prolong the sense that he'd honored her.

''What kinds of boats would you build, if you could?'' she asked.

Phillip walked on for a ways before answering. ''I wanted to build a family sailboat. Not a yacht, not something that cost a half million dollars with every piece of state-of-the-art equipment from microwave oven to radar. Just a simple sailing craft, about thirty feet or so, something to comfortably accommodate a family of four. A boat they could sail together on weekends without a crew. It would have a small cabin including a basic galley for heating a meal and sleeping space for all. It would be efficient, safe and affordable. Most of all, it would be fun.''

She smiled up at him. ''That's a wonderful idea!''

''I'm not sure it's achievable, though.'' He laughed. ''The cost of materials and labor being so high these days, I just don't know.''

''But you could find out. I mean, if you wanted to try again, you could get the information you need and—''

''Alex.''

''Yes?''

''Drop it. It's a fantasy I outgrew a long time ago.''

She hesitated, watching his face closely. His eyes had shimmered with a euphoric glow as he'd told her about the boat of his dreams. The hell he'd outgrown it! That sort of enthusiasm didn't leave a person easily. She'd seen something similar in her father, once or twice over the years, when he was onto a really important deal.

''Are you sure?'' she whispered.

He nodded. ''Besides, we have more important issues to consider now.''

She linked her arm companionably through his. ''Like?''

''Securing our transport for the weekend. And I think I see it right down there.''

Alex followed the line of Phillip's pointing finger to the beach they'd passed earlier. Fewer of the fishing dories remained. Two men sat in the sand, mending nets.

She frowned, more than a little worried. ''We're going to steal a fishing boat?''

He laughed. ''Of course not. We're going to make a trade, if you're willing to sacrifice your shawl.''

She looked at the pastel square, now flung over his

shoulder and bulging with their remaining food. "It's old, and I rarely use it. Sure, why not?" She didn't tell him it was a Gucci, purchased at a chic salon in Rome.

It took less than five minutes for Phillip to complete his bartering with the fisherman. The flowered shawl, which the boat's owner was sure his wife would be delighted to have, for the weekend use of one of his larger boats that sported a makeshift cabin in its center.

The dory was built of wood, looked as if it could use a new coat of paint above the waterline and a good scraping of the hull below to remove the barnacles that encrusted its bottom. But its cozy cabin would provide shelter should it rain. Phillip also assured her that, small as it was, they could sleep inside on blankets provided by their host, thereby avoiding the need to locate a room for the night or sleep in the open on the beach.

When Alex first stepped aboard, after the men had pushed the sturdy craft into the water, the boat smelled like the insides of a tuna fish can. But by the time Phillip had maneuvered it a few hundred feet away from shore, Alex forgot about the briny odor and lost herself in the beautiful scenery. She helped Phillip raise a well-used mainsail, and they skimmed across teal-blue water, beneath an azure sky.

The breeze was light but steady. And once they'd set a smaller, triangular second sail, which he called a jib, they picked up speed and the little boat sliced effortlessly through the low waves. Never had Alex felt so at peace with her surroundings or with herself. The water seemed to sing reassuringly to her: *You can make no wrong decisions…just drift with me…follow your heart…release yourself to the wind.*

"Where are we going?" she asked after a while, though

she didn't particularly care. As long as she was with Phillip on the water, she was content.

"We'll explore a few coves around the west end of the island. By dusk we should anchor for the night. Tomorrow, if you like, we can sail across the channel to the southern coast of Italy and see what we can find for our meals."

"That sounds wonderful," she agreed.

The day was perfect from Alex's perspective. Although she had accompanied friends who cruised Lake Michigan on their parents' luxury motorized or sailing yachts, she herself had never done the work of sailing. There always had been a crew to handle the sails or serve beverages and snacks on deck.

This was more fun. Phillip taught her how to tack to make the most of the wind by changing directions. She held the tiller as he instructed. The surge of water against the tiller blade made it feel as if she were holding the end of a kite string. The vibrations set off by the wind in the sails made the boat feel alive.

She felt alive, too.

As the sun started to set, Phillip aimed the little boat toward a small cove they'd discovered earlier in the day. The land was rocky, rust- and cream-colored patches of stone, as if taken from a Manet painting. A sandy beach formed a white crescent moon. Above were two small villas, one a pastel green, the other a pale-peach hue. There were no people in sight. The cove was as isolated and pristine a spot as she'd ever seen.

"I'm beginning to wish we weren't leaving tomorrow," Alex said as they munched on the remaining bread and cheese for their supper.

"We can stay here, if you like." Phillip moved over to sit closer to her. His arm came around her, and Alex relaxed into its warmth. Kiss me, she thought. Please, please, kiss me.

She needed very badly to be touched in that special way. The man who had kissed her last had betrayed her. Desperately, so very desperately, she wanted to banish all memory of that shattered relationship, all the pain balled up in her heart that had been left there by Robert.

She could think of no better way to do that than by finding a lover to take his place. A man who would so overshadow her fiancé's lingering presence that Robert Marsh would exist as no more than a pale, nearly forgotten shadow over her life.

Phillip was silent for what felt like a long while. He didn't move, didn't seem to be breathing. Alex would give anything to know what he was thinking. She wondered about the night to come. Was it only wishful thinking on her part? Had it even crossed his mind that they might become lovers?

Impulsively, she decided to test the waters.

Lifting her chin, Alex looked back over her shoulder at Phillip. He was staring out across the water, to all appearances lost in distant thought. She was struck by how lovingly his eyes passed over the wave tops, as if he was gentling them with the caress of his gaze. Was he thinking about his dream boat again? Or was she occupying the secret corners of his mind?

Alex planted a soft kiss on the underside of his chin. For a moment Phillip didn't react, then, slowly, his eyes leveled down toward her.

"Maybe you're right."

"About what?" she whispered, her voice strangely hoarse, her heart thudding in her ears.

"Maybe I should try again. Forget everything else. Just build the damn boat."

"Of course you should," she said, pleased and disappointed at the same time. It was nice that he'd taken her advice about pursuing his dream, but upsetting that her kiss hadn't moved him to take advantage of a potentially romantic moment. In the next second, though, she realized that she shouldn't have been so quick to dismiss her chances.

Gradually, his eyes lost their distant look and focused cleanly, sharply, then demandingly on her. He dropped a hand to her face and stroked one finger along her cheek. "You're as lovely as the sunset."

A nervous laugh escaped her lips. "Nice line."

"No," he said, "really. Your face is glowing. The sun and wind, they've brought color to your cheeks."

He touched his fingertip to her lips. She parted them softly and met his gaze. Slowly, he bent down and turned her toward him. Their lips tentatively met, and she felt the warmth of his arms close around her.

His second kiss was longer, deliciously deep, and promised more. The tip of his tongue flicked over her teeth, then probed, coaxing feelings from her that were new and exciting, unlike any she'd felt before. To her surprise, she sensed a delicate moistening, a subtle throbbing between her thighs.

She was eager and ready for him so quickly! He had hardly touched her. Amazing, and a bit frightening.

Alex moved away from him just enough to catch her breath. His eyes were suddenly hot, bright with hunger. The muscles in his biceps where her hands had come to rest were knotted. She could see the desire in his eyes, and knew he would have no trouble reading her responding willingness. But he couldn't possibly know that, although some of these feelings had stirred in her before, she'd had little real experience with sex.

Having attended all-girls' schools through college, she'd had a few boyfriends but no serious relationship until she met Robert. Before that, her parents had seen that she dated only "the right kind of young man." And her brothers had scared off the few young men who had evaded her parents' watchful eyes.

As if that wasn't enough, most of her post-college dates were well aware of who her father was. They cautiously avoided overstepping the bounds of social propriety—which meant they didn't press her to sleep with them.

As a result, she'd slept with only two people—a young man she'd shared a few classes with during her final two years of college, and Robert Marsh. Unlike those who'd been intimidated by her father, Robert had decided to use seduction to get what he wanted. Unfortunately, she'd only seen through him when it was almost too late. He'd been that effective a liar.

Phillip's kisses trailed a line of fire down her throat, wrenching her out of the past and back to the present. She promptly forgot everything but the sensations assaulting her. Marvelous sensations, glorious warmth, all through her body.

Even so, she was nervous, sure that any minute Phillip would realize how little knowledge she possessed of moments like this. Moments when a man and woman stood together on a precipice of desire, making a decision that, ultimately, might bring either joy or despair, pleasure or pain.

"I want you, Alex," Phillip whispered, his voice gravelly with desire. "I hadn't planned this, but now here we are and—"

She pressed the pads of two fingers over his lips. "I know. It's all right."

"It's all right to want you?" He smiled but that didn't

diminish the steely tension in his voice. "Or it's all right to make love to you?"

Suddenly she couldn't breathe. The concept was arousing. But his saying the words sent flames licking through her body. What on earth would his hands, the rest of his body do?

"I meant," she murmured, "the second."

Five

Phillip gently pressed Alex down into the sunken cockpit of the boat. A pile of wool blankets lay beneath her, protecting and cushioning her back from the weathered boards. The high wooden gunwales protected them from view of anyone standing on the shore or passing by the cove by boat.

Alex stared up at Phillip, excited yet afraid. The stars above his head blazed more brilliantly than any over the Chicago cityscape. How very black the firmaments were. How many more stars twinkled. How rapidly her heart beat in her breast. She felt as if she couldn't take another breath without shattering into a million bright shards. Her hands trembled as she lifted them to glide her fingertips through the closely clipped dark hair above Phillip's ears.

It occurred to her that one reason she had agreed to marry Robert was because she had never felt threatened by him during moments of intimacy. He never did any-

thing unexpected. Never made her feel she might be
blinded by passion or risk leaping off an emotional cliff
in a desperate attempt to find love.

Sex had seemed just one part of the bargain a woman
made when she entered marriage. She would sleep in the
same bed as her husband, and he would have access to her
body because that was one of the clauses required by the
deal. And cutting deals was something she knew about,
being Grant Connelly's daughter.

But here, with Phillip Kinrowan, prince of Silverdorn,
she felt swept up in the dark blaze of his tiger eyes. *This*
wasn't a deal, a compromise, or even a polite bargain. *This*
was surrender.

She was alone with a man of power, with a lust for life
and, apparently, for her. He was ready to take her, and she
sensed that the moments to follow would demand that she
respond with every inch of her body and the very essence
of her soul.

Take me! her heart cried out.

Then, almost immediately, she feared she might beg him
to stop. But when his hand touched her breast through the
white gauze of her dress, a need deep inside of her reached
out for him. His strong, wide palm warmed her breast. An
intoxicating heat spread through her limbs. It was a delicious sensation, and she suddenly longed to prolong it.

The urgency of her own desire shocked her. It was the
reverse of struggling to wake from a dream; Alex fought
to hold on to the delicious reverie. She pressed up against
his hand, inviting him to touch her other places, forbidden
places that ached for him.

Phillip gazed down at the woman in his arms. Alex.

Moonlight played off her lovely features. Her green eyes
glittered with gold, reflecting the stars above them. It had
been a long time since he'd slept with a woman, over a

year now. Only one woman had shared his bed since the divorce, and he had counted that weekend as a mistake before it was over.

He had met Angelica in a bar, of all places. She was clearly not his type, and he sensed that she had no lasting interest in him, either. To be honest, he was relieved when the affair ended so quickly, so easily. He hadn't been looking for a serious relationship after the nightmare of his marriage. He wasn't sure he'd ever be capable of trusting so completely, of giving so much of himself again.

But now, with Alex, feelings he could swear he'd never experienced before seized him. It was as if he were the prey instead of the hunter he'd set out to be. He felt powerless to fight these mysterious sensations drawing him toward Alex. Her lovely body, his renegade lust left him no choice.

She was lovely, yes, and clearly she was willing to make love with him. But it was more than that. With her, he didn't fear the age-old traps. She was a hardworking woman who thrived in a tough profession. She had no desire to climb social ladders, collect trophy husbands, or gain an aristocratic title through wedlock. She wasn't looking for a lifelong mate or a sugar daddy to bankroll her taste for expensive jewelry. In short, she wasn't a threat to him.

Thus he could be free of all inhibition and simply experience a delicious sensual adventure with her. In return, he would give her the most pleasure he was capable of giving a woman.

Phillip unfastened the top button of her dress bodice and slid his hand beneath. His palm moved over the warm, soft flesh of Alex's breast. She was silk beneath his fingers, so unexpected for a woman who worked in a demanding environment dressed in leather and denim.

He lowered his head, closed his eyes and dropped a kiss on one tender mound. She squirmed with pleasure beneath him and let out a little sigh he considered ample encouragement. Pressing aside the pale gauze, he saw what his touch had already discovered—she wore no bra. That made her seem all the more brazen and receptive to him.

His lips found a rosy nipple—small, delicate, perfect— and he drew its dainty tip between his teeth and teased the supple flesh until she moaned and pressed her hands around the back of his head and brought him down harder against her.

Greedily he suckled her, savoring the wild motions of her body as she reacted to the measured rasping of his teeth against her skin. It wasn't difficult to slip the elasticized ruffle of her dress off her smooth shoulders. When she lay bare to the waist beneath him, the moonlight flowing over her ivory skin, he could only gaze at her in wonder.

"Please...don't stop," she gasped.

"I'm not stopping, just admiring," he whispered, tracing the contours of her sweet breasts with his fingertips. "I want to take this very slowly. I want this to last a very, very long time."

"I—I'm not sure I'll— Oh, my...I'm not sure *I* will last," she said shakily as he nibbled a tempting hollow at the base of her throat. "I want—" Her eyes levered downward to the front of his pants. "I want *you*."

Phillip chuckled low in his throat, delighted with her. "Be my guest, pretty lady."

To his surprise, her eyes widened and she blushed and hesitated. He thought it charming though odd, she being a woman who had spent her life around nature, that she didn't take sex more casually. Horsewomen, at least in his elevated social circles, had a reputation for being passionate and prolific lovers. If he hadn't known who Alex was, he might have guessed she was relatively new to the game.

Alex drew the tip of her tongue along her top lip, considering Phillip's invitation, then the zipper of his pants. "You mean, you want me to…"

"Do whatever you like," he said, repeating his invitation.

Their eyes met. The effect was electric, but Alex still didn't make her move.

"If you're not sure where to start," he said with mock solemnity, "I have a few suggestions."

She blinked up at him, looking uncertain, the blush returning for an encore. He whispered in her ear.

"Oh my!" She laughed, almost choking on the words.

To help her along, he took her hand, guided it down the front of his khaki pants and pressed her fingers over the rigid proof of his desire. Jade fireworks lit up her eyes as they widened still more. Behind the screen of her long dark lashes, he could see something awakening, something beginning to simmer, and the heat grew rapidly to a blaze.

"I see," she whispered.

The pressure of her hand against him increased, and suddenly the urge to release himself came on so fast, so strong, he had to lift her fingers away for a moment.

He had to catch his breath. Focus on the sky, the waves, anything but her. Force aside the heat, the craving, just for the moment.

There was so much more to be done for Alex before he could allow himself that final race toward ecstasy.

He blocked out his own needs and focused fully on hers. Moving aside the hem of her skirt, he closed his fingers around her slim ankle. Slowly, slowly he slid his hand up her long, elegant leg.

He took his time. Making brief forays with the pads of

his fingers over neighboring terrain. Circling over sensitive spots. Favoring the soft depression at the back of her knee, before moving on. Rising a little higher, an inch at a time, until Alex's breathing sounded ragged, frantic, and her soft sighs plunged to needy female groans.

When he at last reached her lovely thighs, she was writhing beneath him, arching toward him, clutching the muscles stretched tautly over his shoulder blades with frenzied delight. Urging him on with her moans, with the fire in her eyes.

He touched the velvety, moist lips of her womanhood. Caressed and teased and flickered fingertips over her honeyed, yielding flesh. But he did not attempt entry.

"Ah! Oh yes, Phillip!" she cried, the words coming fast and slurred between gasps. "Please... Are you trying to drive me mad?" She grabbed his shoulders.

He grinned at her eagerness, but his own body was responding so fiercely to her arousal, he could barely contain himself. Still, it was fun to torment her, just a little while longer.

"Shall I stop?"

"Don't you *dare,* you crazy man! I need you—" She drew a hissing breath as he circled one finger around the succulent orifice. "Need you *inside* of me!" she specified, as if there might be any question in his mind as to what she wanted.

The gentle rocking of the boat in the night wind intensified each touch, each pressure of skin against skin.

Phillip crushed his mouth over Alex's full lips, kissing her deeply, wantonly, thinking of nothing beyond this moment with her. Needing to breathe, he sat up for just a moment, as moonlight cast long, shimmering streaks of gold across the wave tops.

She seized his belt and yanked him back down, body to

body. He was afraid his weight might hurt her, but she seemed to want him on top of her, all one hundred eighty pounds of man. Who was he to argue? She felt wonderful beneath him, bursting with energy, more naked than dressed, begging for all of him.

Then Phillip remembered. With a violent kick to the gut of regret, he closed his eyes and silently cursed himself.

"Alex, honey," he whispered, "it's been a long time. I hadn't dared to dream you and I...not this soon." Damn it, he couldn't even get the words out. "I'm not totally prepared."

She was fumbling with his belt buckle, tearing the little silver prong out of the hole in the leather, moving hurriedly on to his zipper. "How unprepared is 'not totally'?" Although she stared up at him, her eyes enormous, her fingers were still working feverishly. She pulled down his zipper tab.

He winced in answer.

"You have *no* protection?"

"Nothing," he whispered, intent on doing the right thing by her, even if it meant the agony of not reaching the fiery climax building within his loins even now.

Her eyes closed and she drew a shuddering breath. Her touch softened, but didn't withdraw.

Phillip thought fast. It might not be impossible even under these less than ideal circumstances.

Her hand still stroked the open space that his zipper, moments earlier, had covered. The silky sensation of her fingers smoothing up and down him through his briefs drove him wild. There must be a way. There must!

He had to think clearly. Had to explain to her, and fast. "Listen for just a second. In the last four years I've been only with my wife and one other woman, and in all that time I was fully protected. There's no question in my mind that you're safe with me." He hesitated, for some strange reason not sure he wanted to hear her history. But there was no getting around it if he wanted to finish what he'd started. "Your turn, Alex."

She looked away, as if embarrassed by his directness. "A college friend, a long time ago. Then my fiancé. In both instances, we each were tested before we slept together."

"So," he said guardedly, "we're all right, then?"

She made an adorable face. "There's still the little matter of a pregnancy."

"Ah, yes," he murmured, laying delicate kisses along the rim of her ear. Everything was going to be just fine. More than fine. "But I know how to deal with that. Will you trust me?"

When she pulled back to look up into his eyes, he reassured her with a wink. Alex gave him a skeptical look. "This is fairly important, you realize," she said dryly.

"I promise. I'll make sure you're safe, Alex."

She wondered why that didn't sound like a convenient line. But coming from Phillip, she somehow trusted his intentions as well as his ability to keep his promise. Instinctively, she knew she could leave the details to him, and everything would be all right.

She hooked one finger in the waistband of his briefs, pulling down on the elastic until he was exposed. The length, the breadth and hardness of him made her shudder pleasurably and draw a sharp breath.

"Is this in lieu of a *yes?*" he asked, his voice tight. "Don't just go along with me if you're worried or frightened. I don't want it to be that way between us."

When she at last lifted her gaze again, the bright playfulness in her eyes told him all he needed to know.

Phillip hurriedly pulled down his pants and briefs. Before he could lower himself over her, she reached out and grasped him. He was taut and beautifully shaped, and she could already imagine how he'd feel slipping between her thighs, moving within her. But would he do as he'd promised, protect her from pregnancy?

There was no more time for thought. He was obviously ready for her and she would not stop him now with nervous questions. Something in the steely glint of his usually warm eyes told her there was little short of a scream that would call a halt to this.

He firmly parted her thighs with one muscled knee. She wrapped her arms around his neck and pulled him down on top of her. It took less than a heartbeat for him to find her. Then she felt his shaft, hot and rigid, smooth and unyielding, penetrate her.

All gentleness was gone. Phillip thrust within her hard and deep. Alex relished the strength of him, the demands he made of her. She wouldn't have wanted tenderness at this moment.

This was all about a man claiming a woman, branding her as his own, conquering her and guaranteeing that, if others came after him, she would never forget him or this moment. As remarkable as it seemed, as full and large as he had appeared seconds earlier, he now swelled larger inside of her. She gloried in the sensation.

Phillip nuzzled his lips into the hollow of her throat, kissing her fast and often as they moved together in perfect synchronism. His kisses blazed a fiery path up her neck to her chin, then her lips. She opened her eyes to find him watching her reactions as he thrust again and again. His solemn intensity made her shiver, even as flames licked through her body.

As she locked her long legs around his hips, bringing him harder and harder into her, her breaths came in short, rapid bursts, and his in tortuous rasps. Every part of her body felt flushed, full of him, alive with energy. Every corner of her heart filled to overflowing with joy. She felt intoxicated with heretofore undiscovered passions. With an ardor she'd never dreamed herself capable.

And Phillip.

Phillip seemed to know without being told where all the hidden sensitive places were. Where to kiss, where to touch firmly or caress lightly. Finally she felt herself bloom from within. In a brilliant explosion of color and heat, Alex reached climax upon climax, one following the next in such rapid succession, she was unable to discern where one ended and the next began.

She cried out, tried to silence herself, but couldn't. Never, *never* in her life had she felt this wildness, this ecstasy that Phillip had so expertly drawn from her.

Phillip felt as if he were riding a wildcat. Such a fragile thing Alex had appeared. Yet she was pure dynamite when aroused. As soon as he'd entered her he'd had to fight the almost irresistible drive to allow his own raging bliss to sweep him away. But he'd promised her he'd take no chances with her, and he also instinctively understood that she required more time, more touching before she would be completely satisfied.

At first, he thought he could count each of her climaxes. Her frantic gyrations alternated with throaty warbles of rich satisfaction, marking each feminine release and the brief respites between. But soon there were no valleys between her wild, skyward flights, and he was amazed by her stamina. How freely she allowed her body to take her away, time and again. He watched her and shared in her rapture.

Phillip stayed himself far longer than he believed himself capable. He let her use him, meeting every lovely undulation of her body with his own power. Soon he was glad he had waited. At last, she lay beneath him, limp, sated, open to him. He pressed himself deeply within her one last time. Then hastily he withdrew and allowed himself his own release in a fiery stream between their sweat-soaked bodies.

Such glorious agony. Dying a little, yet living brighter than ever before. Contrasts in reality, yet no less real than the woman beneath him.

Amazingly, as soon as he was spent, the desire returned stronger than ever. Always before, once had been plenty for him. But with Alex, just a glance at her, a soft touch of her hand on his bare hip, the sound of her sigh, and he wanted her again.

Phillip rested only long enough to be sure he was capable of what he imagined. Without moving at all, he felt himself swell again, harden, grow hot. Ramping himself up on his elbows, he looked down to see her reaction, for he knew she must feel him against her.

She said nothing, but the pleased look in her eyes was sufficient answer.

"Really?" she whispered.

"Really," he ground out. "But I don't dare…you know. Too dangerous."

"I know." She wrapped her delicate fingers around him, and it was enough.

His final thought before he drifted off with Alex in his arms was that he'd be a fool to let this woman off the island. If only he could keep her with him, just for a while longer.

Six

Alex woke to the soft sounds of wavelets lapping against the hull of the dory. Gray and white terns glided in an effortless ballet across a cloudless blue sky above her, calling to one another. She stirred, slowly stretching her legs, then her arms.

She was a little stiff from having slept outside but not at all cold. Phillip's body had shaped itself around hers, warming her through the night, as if protecting her not only from the elements but from all possible harm. Even now one muscled arm curled around her waist.

She gently lifted his arm away so that she could sit up and gaze across the azure water of the cove where they'd anchored for the night. Drawing a deep breath, she closed her eyes and savored the salty air, the gentle rocking motion of the boat, the feeling that she'd left everything behind her that could ever again make her unhappy.

Incredible.

"Where's breakfast?" a deep voice rumbled up at her from the bottom of the boat.

"Don't you remember? We ate the last of our provisions for supper."

Food was the last thing on her mind at the moment.

"I remember nothing of last night," Phillip grumbled, dropping one arm across his eyes to shield them from the brilliant morning sun. He was teasing her, and she loved it.

"Nothing?" she cooed, trailing a fingertip down the center of his chest. She circled one masculine nipple through the rich jungle of hairs.

He grabbed her hand and pulled her down on top of him. "Something *is* coming back to me." His amber eyes glowed in the morning light. "How about refreshing my memory?"

Smiling, she bent down and kissed him on the mouth. Once, twice, then a third time, longer, deeper. She decided she enjoyed his morning flavors as well as she had his nighttime ones.

His hands moved over her body, beneath the loose cotton dress she'd pulled back on for sleeping, as she'd felt nervous about sleeping in the nude. However unlikely, someone might have come by in another boat. Phillip played with her breasts, licked her nipples, and in no time at all she was eager for him again.

Then, just as quickly he stopped and knelt above her.

"What's wrong?" she gasped.

"Nearly forgot." He rolled his eyes in exaggerated dismay. "Woman, we have to get ashore and buy some protection. I want to come inside of you so badly I don't know how much longer I can take it."

She laughed, delighted, although she too ached for him. He was capable of bringing her so high, so fast, it amazed her. Their eyes met with sudden understanding. She smiled and nodded. Phillip reached for her and pulled her back into his arms.

"Touch me," he whispered in her ear. "Touch me the way you did last night, Alex, and I'll make sure you don't start your day restless."

She giggled, feeling deliciously wicked. "Deal."

Her fingers reached down to him, as he moved his wide, gloriously warm palm between her thighs. Moments later, Phillip's sensitive touch dredged up from within her a delicious rush of heat and she returned the favor. She smiled with satisfaction at the expression of pure pleasure that came over his handsome features.

Afterward, they dozed beneath the morning sun, contentedly considering their options for the day.

"You know, I really am hungry now," Phillip murmured.

"Then we'd better set sail," Alex said. "Where to? Still the Italian coast?"

He nodded, pushing himself up to step into pants before unfastening the sail covers. "Taranto is the nearest point of mainland to Altaria. Should take us a little over an hour. We can have breakfast, then walk around town, restore our water supply, buy something for lunch if we can find someplace that's open on Sunday and be back at the villa by nightfall."

Alex frowned. It was as if his words had cast a cloud over the dazzling summer sun. "We can't spend another night in the dory?"

He looked pleased that she asked. "The owner wants her back in time for fishing early Monday morning. That means on the beach and loaded with bait and equipment before 5:00 a.m."

"I see." She had missed that part of the negotiations,

Alex realized, as it had been carried out in the local patois of the island. She felt sorry that their experiment would end so soon.

Phillip bent down to drop a consoling kiss on the tip of her nose then began to raise the mainsail.

His bare chest and shoulders gleamed a smooth tan in the sunshine as he walked deftly to the bow. The muscles of his arms and back alternately knotted and flexed as he reached down and hauled back the anchor chain. She admired the masculine contours and longed to trace a finger along each sexy bulge and hollow. Perhaps tonight, at his estate, she would feel his sinews move beneath her hands as he supported himself above her. As they made love yet again.

This could get addictive, she thought.

"You're awfully quiet all of a sudden," he commented as he dragged the iron anchor out of the water. "Disappointed?"

No, she wasn't disappointed. "Oh, about leaving the dory?" Of course that was what he'd meant. She chuckled to herself. "I just thought it was nice last night sleeping under the stars. Then there was the lack of pressure to compete with anyone, money no longer being an issue."

"I had supposed roughing it might be something you'd be more accustomed to than I was." He studied her face for a moment, as if puzzled by her comment. "You know, privileged life and all, in my case."

"Of course," she said quickly, realizing how close she'd come to totally slipping out of her role. "We used to camp out all the time, Mom, Dad and me."

She was adlibbing recklessly now, but it seemed necessary at the time. Although creating more tales was inevitably taking her further from an opportunity for telling him the truth. Even as Alex further embellished her story, she regretted her runaway imagination, which seemed to have taken control of her mouth.

"But that was in the state park, back in Illinois. I've never slept on a boat before." That last part, at least, was true.

"If you liked it so much, we'll have to do it again someday. How long do you have before you leave Altaria?"

She dropped her gaze guiltily to her hands in her lap. "I'm not sure exactly. It depends."

Lord knew she'd left a mess at home, running out on her wedding as she had. Her poor parents must have made a ton of apologies and excuses on her behalf. It couldn't have been easy for them.

Then there were all those wedding gifts. What had become of them?

Probably they were still on display in her mother's sitting room on the twin mahogany tables, each with its tiny engraved card to identify the giver. More important things would be on Grant's mind, at least. Like trying to figure out who had tried to kill her brother, after murdering her uncle and cousin. Who and why?

"Depends?" Phillip echoed her nonexplanation.

"On the Connellys," she said quickly.

"Of course. I haven't had a chance to meet the American branch of the royal family, other than the king and his queen. They seem like good people," he said solemnly.

"They are," she said. I love them very much.

But she couldn't say that last part aloud. And although he'd brought up the subject of her family, it seemed awkward to just blurt out the truth now. She'd played her charade too well. Phillip was bound to be offended if, so soon after her latest decoration of her story, she admitted to him that she was lying, and had been doing so from the moment they'd met.

Besides, everything had changed now. Events had somehow been removed from her control. She and Phillip weren't just acquaintances now. They were *lovers*. And lovers ought not to deceive each other. Robert had lied to her and used her. That was why she'd left him. How could she blame Phillip if he walked out on her, when she was doing the same thing to him?

Alex felt physically ill at the thought. Finding herself looking at a future without Robert had been a painful experience, but losing Phillip, even before they had sorted out their true feelings for each other, might well destroy her.

"Well, let's just enjoy this day," he was saying as she put confusing thoughts away for later. He pulled on the halyards, and the big weather-yellowed sail flapped, climbing slowly up the mast on wooden rings that clacked merrily in the breeze. She watched the sail fill with wind, felt the boat respond and begin to move again, coming to life.

"Yes," she said, shading her eyes to meet Phillip's as a gentle sadness tugged at her heart. "There's at least today."

The ache in her shoulder that had plagued her since her fall from Eros had been forgotten last night, but the early morning dampness started it hurting again. She gently rolled her shoulder, easing the muscles, then sat where the sun could warm the joint. Soon the hurt subsided and she lifted her face to the wind and delighted in the smooth, silent glide of the dory as it cut through the glistening water.

They sailed north then west toward the heel of the Italian boot. In another forty-five minutes she spotted a low, gray ribbon of land.

Phillip sat in the stern of the boat, tiller in one hand, his other arm wrapped around her. Alex had positioned herself between his long legs, leaning back against his chest, gazing at the horizon as it came closer and closer. Before long she could make out stately cedars and pines, stretching high above a cliff. Rocky ledges dropped down to the water's edge.

"How will we get ashore?" she asked. "There doesn't seem to be very good anchorage close to land, or a beach. Do we swim?"

"We'll sail around the bluff and into the bay. There are two or three sandy beaches farther along from here. We'll pick one and sail the boat right up onto the sand. You won't even get your pretty feet wet."

Phillip studied Alex from above her head. Her cheeks had turned a lovely pink in the wind and sun, and her short, dark hair was ruffled and wild-looking. But there was something fragile about her that he hadn't noticed before they'd made love. Something that didn't fit a young woman who made her living disciplining animals that outweighed her ten or more times over.

When he'd laced his fingers through hers and spread her arms wide as he'd moved within her, he'd sensed how very smooth and soft her palms were. Not calloused and toughened by leather reins, as he might have thought.

In fact, from the moment he'd met her that night at the palace, he'd thought something was not quite right about her. It hadn't been a strong impression then, more of a subtle tweak of doubt. But the tweaks had become more frequent and stronger with time.

Last night and this morning he'd glimpsed underlying traits in Alex that made little sense to him—a vulnerability, an inexperience, a suspicion that sex was newer to her than she let on. These things just didn't jibe with the earthy, physically adept woman he'd believed he'd met that first night. He wondered if she was keeping something from him. Some part of her life that he should know about, now that they'd become intimately involved. But something made him reticent to ask.

"Look, there's a beach. About eleven o'clock," Alex chirped, interrupting his darkening thoughts. "If we land there, do you suppose a town is close enough to walk to?"

"Looks good to me."

He wondered, was he just being nosy by wanting to know more about her? He wanted to ask her questions, lots of them. But he also didn't want to spoil their perfect day together. Besides, he was probably digging for no reason. Why couldn't a woman who worked with horses have soft hands, if she took care to moisturize them? Why should Alex fit a stereotype he'd created for her profession?

She was her own person, and an American, with different ways of behaving and thinking than the European women he'd met. Why couldn't he relax and simply enjoy the magic of being with her?

Because, he answered his own question, *you've been wrung out and hung up to dry before.* Despite his attraction to the opposite sex, women somehow had become the enemy. It was damn hard to trust anyone as pretty and interesting as Alex.

Nevertheless, he tried to put his concerns out of mind as the boat rushed toward the golden beach on a billow of air. "We're moving at about six knots," he said, "too fast for coming into shore."

"What do we do?" she asked. "It's not like we have a motor you can throw into reverse."

He smiled. "True. We take down the jib, lessen the push the wind has on the boat. Here, take the tiller. You steer while I lower the sail."

She looked hesitant, but took his place and held the tiller steady while he moved forward in the boat.

"Keep us pointed toward that pink villa a little to your right. Move your hand to the right to turn left, to the left to turn right. The opposite of steering a car."

She smiled like a child who has been introduced to a new and exciting game. "I think I can do that."

Phillip watched her out of the corner of his eye as he took in the jib then reefed the mainsail to slow them down. She was experimenting with the tiller, trying to find just the right angle to compensate for wind and waves and to keep them on course. She caught on fast, and her delighted smile told him she was enjoying herself.

Meanwhile, he watched their approach. At just the right moment, he dropped the mainsail to the deck, cutting off the wind so that they would drift the last hundred feet to the beach. The hull scraped the shallow bottom of the cove. He rolled up his pant legs and jumped into calf-deep water and pulled the boat the rest of the way onto dry sand. Alex stepped out of the boat and eagerly looked around.

"You're sure this is Italy?" she asked. "I mean, it's not like there are any signs telling you where we are. We could be anywhere."

"Trust me, this is Italy. Ever been here before?"

She seemed hesitant before answering, which he thought was strange. "Florence, years ago."

"Ah, Firenza, yes," he said. "For the All-Europe equestrian competitions?"

"Yes," she agreed quickly, but her eyes didn't meet his. "Um, which way is Taranto?"

He frowned at her obvious shift of topic. She seemed eager to avoid talking about her work, and he wondered why. "This way." He scooped up the water jug from the bottom of the boat. "We'll need to fill this."

They walked for nearly a mile before coming to a village at the outskirts of Taranto.

Each simple shop along the cobbled vias specialized in one or two items. The *panetteria* for bread, where rough wooden planks lined stone walls that would keep the loaves cool even on a hot summer's day. The *macelleria* for fresh sausage and meats. Cheeses of many varieties were displayed in another window, and the *drogheria* offered a variety of fruits, vegetables and packaged goods. The only problem was, all the shops they passed were closed on this Sunday morning. But they found a small restaurant where the owner agreed to sell them provisions from his kitchen. They purchased enough food for two meals, filled their water jug and still had a whole dollar left.

"Should we buy pastries for dessert, or save our money for an emergency?" he asked before they left the restaurant.

Alex sighed. "I'm dying for something chocolate, but with the better part of the day left I'd be nervous with no money at all. Better save it."

"A sensible decision." He grinned in approval.

The women he'd grown up around would have spent his last lira in a minute. Alex understood the value of hard-earned cash, and he respected her all the more for that thrifty streak.

They walked back to the boat then spent the afternoon investigating the shoreline from the water, stopping to chat with fishermen now and then. For as long as Phillip could remember, he hadn't felt this relaxed, this happy.

It was dusk before they sailed back into the sheltered cove on Altaria where they'd traded for the boat. Phillip regretfully turned over the dory to the fisherman they'd borrowed it from. He felt more than a little sad at leaving behind such a sturdy little boat.

It was a far cry from the sleek, modern yachts he'd sailed all of his life. Even his experiment with plain, functional boat design seemed unnecessarily luxurious compared to the fishing boats of the island. The dory brought him back to basics, back to his love of the water and with the freedom and challenge it bestowed on all who sailed.

As they walked into his villa's foyer, a manservant met Phillip at the door. "*La signorina* Alex has a telephone message, from the United States. The caller, he say it is *urgente.*" He handed Alex a slip of paper with numbers written on it.

She looked down at it and, as Phillip stood by, her wind-flushed cheeks faded to a chalky gray. "Oh."

"What's wrong?" he asked.

"I'm not sure. This is my father's number, in Chicago. I should call right away."

He nodded. "Use my office. You'll have privacy there if you shut the door."

Alex smiled gratefully at him, feeling guilty because, without even trying to, she was adding another level of deception to their relationship. That was, if they had a relationship and the weekend hadn't been just a fling for Phillip.

Nothing about it felt flinglike to her. What they had shared together seemed real, substantial, important. She hoped she wasn't reading too much into the weekend, or into the man.

They had made amazing love together. She shivered pleasurably at recalled sensations, but firmly pushed them aside. If her father had gone to the trouble of tracking her down here at a stranger's house, his call must be of vital importance.

She plucked the entire telephone off the inlaid surface of the massive dark wood desk. Dropping down on a couch at the opposite end of the book-lined room from Phillip's desk, she set the phone in her lap. Alex dialed the summer house on the lake, having recognized the number there.

Grant himself answered.

"Daddy, it's Alexandra. I'm sorry I couldn't get right back to you. I was traveling and out of touch for a couple of days."

"It's all right, dear. We were just worried about you. At first, no one at the palace seemed to know where you were. Then Daniel explained about your riding accident and about the horse's owner taking you in. Are you sure you shouldn't come home now and have our physician take a look at that shoulder?"

A shadow passed across the window to Alex's left, distracting her for a second. She turned, expecting to see someone, but no one was there. She frowned, puzzled. Had somebody been watching her through the window and quickly moved off before she could see them?

Had it been Phillip? she wondered. But he didn't seem the type to spy on her. If he wanted to know what her call was about, he would have asked.

Her father was speaking and she tried to focus on his words, but an uneasy feeling stayed with her. Someone most definitely had been in that window a moment ago, someone who hadn't wanted to be seen.

"After you left town so quickly," Grant continued, "we were all pretty upset. But your mother and I have wondered if you might want to come home and discuss your future more calmly...or if you might have had second thoughts about Robert."

"Not a one," she said sharply, then regretted taking out the instant flare of anger brought on by her fiancé's name, on her father. "I'm sorry, Daddy, it hasn't been easy. I thought I knew him, but I didn't."

"You've never explained why you called off the wedding."

It was true. She'd left a vague note saying there wasn't going to be a wedding. She could destroy Robert Marsh's career by telling her father the whole truth right now. He'd fire the jerk without batting an eye. But revenge wasn't her style.

"I just realized that his job meant more to him than I did," she said quietly. Which was, after all, the truth. Climbing toward a directorship in her father's company had inspired his romantic fervor. It hadn't mattered whether she had blond hair or black, was short or tall, had a brain in her head. She was simply a vehicle.

"Your mother can attest to my being a workaholic, too," Grant offered gently. "If you love each other, you find ways to—"

"No, Daddy. It wasn't like that. I just…I don't love Robert. I don't suppose I ever did."

"I see." He coughed once, then again. "Well, we won't go into further details on that subject. You sound as if, at least now, you know your own mind. We're here to support you, dear, whatever you decide to do next."

Alex smiled. If she knew nothing else, it was that her heart didn't belong to Robert Dexter Marsh of Chicago. She was saving it for someone else. A man who loved her for who she was, whatever that might someday be.

"Thank you," she said. "For the time being I'm happy to be learning a lot about myself, very quickly, too."

"Good." There was a brief pause on the other end of the line. Then Grant spoke again. "I actually have another reason for calling you, Alex. Since the attempt on your brother's life, you know how careful we've all had to be. Until we find the person who tried to kill him and the reason behind it, we must be vigilant.''

A warning tingle raced up her spine. "Has something happened at home? Is everyone all right?"

"We're all fine," Grant assured her, but his tone was ominous and she thought she heard a desperate tiredness underlying his words. "I just wanted to pass along news of some odd things happening here, to keep you informed, just in case."

"Tell me about it," she said tightly. "I half suspect that someone has been following me here in Altaria."

"Then be sure you're never alone, and stay with people you know and trust. This Phillip Kinrowan, your host, is he a man to be relied upon? Do you know enough about him to put your life in his hands, Alexandra?"

"He's okay, Daddy. He'd never hurt me." But was that true? Did she really know Phillip or was she just saying that because it was what she wanted to believe?

"All right, then," Grant muttered. "But I'd feel better if you were at the palace with ample security. Daniel is worried about you, too, you know. I think he believes your breakup with Robert might cause you to do something foolish."

"I'll stop in and see him," she promised.

"Good." He gave an audible sigh. "One last thing. Just so you know, my assistant, Charlotte, you remember her?"

"Of course," Alex said.

"Well, she's been acting strangely lately. I'm beginning to suspect she's up to something she shouldn't be, and if it has anything to do with this family or the company…" He let the thought go. "At any rate, I'm having Starwind and Reynolds, our investigators, follow her. I can't tell you how deeply this troubles me. I've always thought Charlotte was a loyal employee, but I can't afford even a small leak during the investigation.''

"I know, Daddy. I'm sure even Charlotte would understand, given the circumstances. We all have to be careful.''

She slid her gaze around to the window again, but nothing was there. Then, fleetingly, she thought of Phillip. He required a different sort of caution, didn't he? She'd trust him with her life. But should she trust him with her heart?

Seven

Phillip walked through the stables early the next morning, still feeling the warmth of Alex's body pressed up against his. The previous night when he and Alex had returned from their experiment in frugality, neither of them had spoken of sleeping arrangements. After sipping brandies by the fire in his library, cuddled up on the divan, they'd strolled hand in hand to his bedroom as if by silent agreement. There they made slow, luscious love and fell asleep in each other's arms. It had seemed the natural thing to do after the intimacy of their weekend together.

In the morning when Cook brought him his coffee, there was a second cup and scone on the tray, along with sliced strawberries and a bowl of rich clotted cream. How the woman knew that his relationship with Alex had changed he didn't dare to ask. Perhaps she'd first stopped at Alex's room, found her bed empty then made the correct assumption.

Whatever, they were now together, the household seemed to know it, and, to Phillip's amazement, he welcomed this new development in his life.

Never had he greeted a morning so happily. As if in direct contrast to his present mood, he recalled a reckless weekend a year or more ago. In hindsight, it had been a mistake. But he'd been so terribly lonely, and Angelica, a woman from the other side of the island, had seemed equally in need of companionship. Someone to talk to, to touch if only for a night or two.

The mornings when they'd awakened together had been awkward. That Monday, he'd been honest with her and apologized if he'd led her to believe that he was interested in anything more than sharing a few nights with her. To his relief, she had taken his dismissal with a shrug and left after Cook had fed her a hearty breakfast. He hadn't heard from or seen her since.

But there was something odd about the way they'd met, Phillip mused as he crossed the yard toward the house again. And something unnerving about the way Angelica had moved through his house during those two days, taking in the furnishings, paintings, even the flowers in his garden with a possessive eye. Women like that made him nervous.

No, more than nervous. They terrified him. How long had it taken him to see through his wife? How easy it had been for other women to portray themselves in a way that appealed to a man, then turn around and be another person entirely once they had trapped him into marriage.

The bitterness he'd thought he had left behind returned with a ferocity that shocked him. Why now? Why when he was safe from deceit and feminine wiles? Perhaps it was just that the habit of being suspicious was so hard to break.

Phillip cracked open the door to the library and looked inside. Alex was curled up on his couch, deeply involved in a book she'd pulled from his shelf. She was such a wonderfully different sort of female, so easy to understand. She came from simple beginnings and expected so little from him. She was a dedicated and gifted trainer. Her love of horses was evident in the way she spoke to and touched them in his stables. Alex was pure and honest and good. And, he was sure, she would never ask anything of him he couldn't willingly give. That made her very special indeed. That made her safe to be around a man like him whose wealth and title had proven so tempting to others.

He silently closed the door, leaving her to enjoy her book, and returned to the foyer where mail and phone messages from the weekend lay waiting for him. After sorting through the envelopes, he lifted the small leather-bound book that served as a telephone log. Dr. Elgado had called, checking on his patient. A contractor who was supposed to give him a bid on repairing several stalls in the north stable had tried to reach him. There was a formal invitation to a reception at the palace in two weeks. He would, of course, bring Alex as his date, if she liked and was still in Altaria. And his lawyer had called twice. He didn't know what that could be about; there was no message other than a mention that it was important and he should return the call as soon as possible.

"Phillip?"

He turned with a smile to Alex who had come up behind him without his hearing her footsteps. She'd marked her place in the book with a finger held between the pages.

"Good morning, again," he murmured. Kissing her on the cheek, he lifted a stray wisp of ebony hair off her forehead, which was furrowed in concentration. "Something wrong? Your shoulder bothering you?"

"No, nothing like that." She glanced behind her toward the library. "Last night, while I was calling home—" She hesitated. "It's probably nothing, but was anyone working outside the house, maybe on the grounds nearby?"

He shook his head. "It was dark by that time. Why?"

"I don't know. It's just that as soon as we came back here, I felt as if someone was watching me. There was a moment when, through the office window, while I was talking to my father..." She shrugged.

Phillip frowned. "I don't see how that could be. Or why."

She parted her lips as if she was about to say something more, but stopped herself.

"What is it, Alex? Is something wrong?" Why did he suddenly feel that she wasn't just confused or frightened by whatever she'd imagined or thought she'd seen? Why did he get the feeling she might intentionally be keeping something from him? "Do you have to return to Chicago sooner than you thought?"

"No, no, it's not that." She chewed her bottom lip. Her green eyes looked troubled. "Listen, there's something I need to tell you, something important I should have said to you days ago."

A warning tingle raced through his veins. The urgency in her voice was real and sharp. What could she have kept from him that would make her so jumpy? She gazed beseechingly up at him, and his heart stopped.

She's married, he speculated, and something inside of him died a little. He had been attracted to married women before. Some had even made it clear they were more than willing to ignore their vows to pursue an affair with him. But he had never allowed himself to become involved with a married woman.

He felt a desperate anger surge within him. "The story

about leaving your fiancé at the altar…that was a lie.'' He ground out the words between clenched teeth. He said it aloud this time. ''You're married, aren't you?''

''No, no,'' she said quickly, ''all that's true! And I'm glad I did leave Robert, because if I hadn't I wouldn't have met you!''. Tears clung to her lashes.

Phillip longed to reach out and dash them away, to draw her into his arms and comfort her. But a heavy feeling down low in his gut told him he wasn't going to like what she was about to say next. He stepped forward and seized her by the shoulders.

''Then what is it, Alex?''

''I…my name isn't—''

The front door swung open and in strode Barnaby Jacobs, his lawyer. Phillip spun to meet him, scowling at the interruption. ''What *is* it, Barnaby?'' he snapped impatiently.

''Guess you've already heard if you're in *that* kind of mood,'' Jacobs commented with a wry smile. Phillip somehow knew the pinched tug on the man's lips wasn't meant to convey humor.

Then the lawyer's glance took in Alex. ''Sorry, didn't realize you had a guest, my friend.''

''Heard what?'' Phillip barked.

Barnaby frowned at Alex. ''This young lady isn't by any chance the one who—?''

''Alex Anderson. She's a trainer from the Connelly party, visiting the palace. Alex,'' he said, turning to her, ''meet Barnaby Jacobs, my attorney, and oldest friend, who seems to have forgotten his manners as well as lost his ability to explain himself.''

''Sorry. I'm just glad— Oh, never mind.'' The man still made no sense but he sounded relieved. His pale gray eyes flickered to Alex, then back to his client. He removed a straw hat from his head and held it, along with his brief-case, between two hands in front of him. "Listen, Phillip, we need to talk and it can't wait."

Phillip raked his fingers through his hair. "Suddenly it seems that everyone has crucial news to share."

Barnaby looked puzzled. "I don't understand."

"Never mind. Come on, both of you, into the library where we can talk without the whole household hearing us."

Phillip watched Alex as she walked ahead of him. She didn't look like herself. All the sparkle had left her pretty eyes, and she seemed deep in thought.

It would figure, the one woman he'd have liked to stay with for more than a night or two, and *she* was having second thoughts about *him*. Damn it to hell! What had he been thinking getting involved with her? He'd known she was only going to be in Altaria for a few weeks at the most. But there was something more to her sudden change in attitude toward him. He could sense it.

"All right," Phillip said, rounding on the two of them, "age before beauty. Out with it, Barnaby."

The lawyer set his briefcase on the coffee table and waved Phillip to a chair. "On second consideration, it appears you haven't heard the news. So you'll be better off sitting down."

"If it's that bad, I'll stand, thank you." He shot Alex a puzzled look, still wondering what had been on her mind that had upset her so. What was the woman so afraid of admitting to him?

"Are you sure you don't want this to be more private?" Jacobs asked, clearly with Alex in mind.

"Just get on with it."

"All right." The attorney opened his briefcase and took

out a sheaf of papers. "The short of it is, a young woman claims you're the father of her baby."

Phillip stared at the man, then at the papers in his attorney's hand. "What? You're saying I've been named in a paternity suit?"

"Exactly." Barnaby took a pair of reading glasses from his case and perched them on the tip of his bulbous nose. He consulted the pages before him. "A Ms. Angelica Terro affirms that you and she had an affair on or about the tenth of January of last year—"

"Two bloody nights, over a year ago!" Phillip roared, avoiding Alex's astonished gaze. He seriously regretted having involved her in this discussion. "I met the woman in a bar. It was stupid. I was lonely and upset, and she was there. End of story."

"Not precisely the end, apparently. You did sleep with her, right?" Barnaby asked, his tone grave.

"Yes, yes, I slept with her. But I used protection. If she's pregnant, it's not by me. I swear it!"

"You're absolutely certain about that? Because her lawyer claims that she—"

"I don't give a blazing fig what anyone claims! I did the responsible thing. I didn't leave her with a baby. If she actually has a child, then it's someone else's!" Phillip was uncomfortably aware of Alex watching him, her face twisted with emotions he couldn't read.

What she might be thinking of him he didn't dare imagine. It wasn't as if he made a habit of bedding strange women. And he certainly had never been irresponsible where children were concerned.

Alex stepped forward. "Listen, this is none of my business. I think I'd better leave you two to sort things out." Her voice was soft, breathless and rushed, as if she couldn't wait to get out of the room. "I'll be out in the stable, Phillip, if you need me."

"It's not the way it looks," he assured her grimly.

She nodded but said nothing more. Her eyes slid away from his when he tried to reassure her with a pleading glance.

"I tried to tell you she shouldn't be here," Barnaby murmured, not unkindly, as soon as Alex had closed the door behind her.

"It's all right. We'll work things out. In the meantime, let's just ignore this preposterous accusation." He moved to the window and stared out thoughtfully over the rich expanse of his gardens. "Hopefully, Ms. Terro will realize she doesn't have the means to prove her claim."

Barnaby sighed. "It's not that easy. If you don't fight her charge, you'll make things more difficult for yourself in the long run."

Phillip turned to glare at him. "Why the hell is that? I'm innocent of any wrongdoing except taking part in a physical act between two consenting adults. Last time I heard, that wasn't illegal."

Barnaby Jacobs fixed him with his sternest, most paternal expression. His heavy gray eyebrows lowered over eyes that had seen everything. He was, in fact, old enough to be Phillip's father, and sometimes he thought of the younger man as he would have had he had a son. "What I *meant* was, if you don't fight the suit, it's as if you're admitting your guilt."

"That's ridiculous!" Phillip threw up his hands and paced away from then back toward the windows. "Be straight with me. Do you think this is some sort of confidence game to get money out of me? Or—" he rounded on Barnaby so sharply the other man fell back a step "—is this young woman in some sort of trouble and she's so desperate for help she's been forced to lie to get it? If she's in serious difficulties, I'm perfectly willing to give her a hand.''

Barnaby sighed and rested a calming hand on Phillip's shoulder. "You're too generous, dear friend. Giving her money now could well lock you into paying her off until this child turns twenty-one, or even longer. This is serious. This is something that could follow you for the rest of your life.''

Phillip felt his gut tighten up inside. Of all the times for something like this to happen. He was just getting to know Alex. Just beginning to think there might be a special connection between them that should be nurtured. What would she think of him now?

"All right, so I take a blood test, right? Or a DNA test. When there's no match between myself and the child, that will solve the problem.''

"And, what if it comes out positive?'' Barnaby was studying Phillip in a way Phillip didn't like.

"You think I'm lying?''

Their eyes met—the older man studying the other, judging him. "No, of course I don't believe you'd lie, but I don't want to take any chances, either. Let's hold off on the DNA and see if I can get her attorney to back off. Maybe if I threaten a countersuit, or just use the DNA test as a threat.'' He shoved the papers back into his leather attaché. "I'll be in touch as soon as I know anything. In the meantime—'' he glanced meaningfully toward the door through which Alex had disappeared "—you might consider toning down your social life, at least for a while.''

"Don't lecture me, Barnaby,'' Phillip warned. "I'm not spreading my seed around with abandon. Aside from that, Alex isn't the kind of woman who'd take advantage of a man. She's as straight as they come.'' But a twinge of doubt made him wince just a little. Clearly, *something* had been bothering her.

"I hope you're right. You're a mighty tempting target. The kind of money that runs in your family can make even a good woman think twice about using her charms in clever ways."

Phillip made no comment. It wasn't as if the same thought hadn't crossed his own mind. But it was one that he hoped with all his heart had no basis in reality.

Alex had stopped outside the library door and listened, just for a moment. One of the male voices inside mentioned a blood test, the other refused. She assumed that was Phillip—and that wasn't a good sign. She walked as fast as she could to the stables after leaving Phillip to continue consulting with his lawyer.

She had felt awkward and embarrassed, hearing them discuss another woman's intimacies with the man to whom she'd given her body and probably a good deal more. Her heart ached as she'd listened to them. She couldn't tell what Phillip was thinking or feeling, except that he'd looked very angry. Angry and dangerous.

He wasn't a man to be crossed, she was sure of that much. He was powerful and knew how to protect himself. Beneath his anger at the accusations of his former lover, she'd sensed a ruthlessness she'd never have guessed was there.

No, she didn't like thinking about crossing Phillip Kinrowan. Apparently, Angelica Terro had done just that, and he'd left her. Now he was trying to dismiss not only her but the existence of a baby that might well be his.

Was he telling the truth about their being together just two nights? Despite his denials, might Angelica's baby be his? Maybe the affair lasted longer than he'd admitted.

Maybe it was finding out Angelica was pregnant that had sent him running. It wouldn't be the first time imminent parenthood had panicked a man.

But Alex felt strongly about parents being responsible for their children. Deadbeat dads were the dregs of society as far as she was concerned. It made the situation far worse if Phillip, as wealthy as he was, refused to support his own child. But, she reminded herself as she stroked Eros's coal-black mane, so far there was no solid proof that the woman's claims were true.

She felt sickened at another unexpected thought.

What if *she* and Phillip had made a baby while they were making love? What if despite their being careful... No, she wouldn't even consider that possibility! But what if, a voice inside her head asked insistently. What if, either last weekend or in the future she accidentally became pregnant? Would his reaction be as violent as it had been today? Obviously the man wasn't interested in any woman who sought to tie him down to marriage.

So why had she been contemplating lingering in Altaria? Her motive for remaining here was no longer to escape from Robert. Her shoulder was nearly mended. She was perfectly capable of traveling anywhere in the world she wished. Why did she want to stay with Phillip if there was no future for them?

Her temples throbbed from the effort to think, and her neck ached with tension.

Because, she told herself, *you've done the worst possible thing. You've fallen for the man you duped.*

It didn't matter that it had started out as an innocent prank, a private parlor trick at a party, a fantasy that had run away with her. After suffering through the deceptions of a wife who had used him and a former lover who seemed to be trying to do the same thing, what would his reaction be when she told him that she was a wealthy socialite not the lowly horse trainer she'd pretended to be?

Alex shuddered at the thought. Her hand stroked the horse's neck one more time, then she heard footsteps behind her. Before she could turn, Phillip's voice came to her.

"Sorry you had to wait so long, Alex. What was it you wanted to tell me?"

Eight

Alex spun around to face Phillip. His expression was strained, and his features seemed to have a hard edge to them that made her uneasy. "I thought I might find you out here." He reached for her hand.

Involuntarily she cringed. How could she want to be with him, yet at the same time be afraid of him? She might have tricked him, even lied to him, but she had never intended to hurt him. Besides, if what she heard was true, he was guilty of so much worse. Abandoning a child and its mother was not something she, at least, could take lightly.

"Is something wrong, Alex?"

She stared at him as if he were a stranger. "I'd say so." Her throat felt tight and aflame with emotions she barely kept in check. "You have an affair with a woman, leave her pregnant, then try to evade your responsibility as a father." Hot tears flooded her eyes. Her hands trembled at her sides. "That's as wrong as life gets."

He scowled, his eyes revealing nothing. "Is *that* what you think of me?"

"No, I mean…well, yes. That's what I heard in there."

"Alex, I—" He seemed about to say more, but then decided better of it. The muscles in his throat and jaw tightened to ridges. She could almost read his thoughts. Pure male stubbornness won out over reason. "What I do with my personal life is none of your business."

His cruel words broke in a frigid wave over her, bringing her up short. He was right. She had no claim on him. All they'd shared was a handful of nights. They barely knew each other. He, certainly far less than he imagined, thanks to her charade. A horse trainer! How had she ever managed to pull that one off?

Alex shook her head sadly. "I suppose you feel you don't love the woman, and therefore you needn't love her child. But it's your child, too, Phillip."

"No, it isn't." His eyes burned darkly as he lunged toward her, but she darted away from him. "Alex, will you just listen to me for one moment?"

"If the baby isn't yours, why don't you prove it? Why not take a blood test and—"

His groan cut her off. "Stop it, Alex. I didn't do anything wrong, certainly nothing to hurt you!" He reached for her again.

She backed away, shivering at the thought of his touch. The same touch that had given her so much pleasure only hours before.

"I might be her at another time," she whispered shakily. "That's what I kept thinking as I heard you deny your paternity. What if I became pregnant, Phillip? What then?

Would you run just as fast? Would you leave me to raise our baby, and—''

Tears flowed down her cheeks. She didn't know what was the matter with her. She never got this emotional about anything. Even Robert's betrayal hadn't hurt this badly. Then, she'd managed to hide the pain inside. This was different. This struck deep at the heart of her womanhood. A man might desert her, but to deny their child his protection would be past pardoning.

"You're not listening to me, Alex. I told you I'm not the father, dammit. And as far as the DNA test—'' He didn't know why he couldn't just explain that it was he who wanted the test, and his lawyer who had advised against it. For some reason, he balked at having to defend himself to Alex. They had been as close as a man and woman could be. She should know him by now!

It hurt that she could be so wrong about him. To accuse him of insensitivity at least and neglect of his own child at the very worst, well, that meant she didn't trust him. She had weighed his word against that of a stranger, and had decided to accept the stranger's. How was that fair? It didn't matter what little bit she heard, she should have believed in him. That is, if she was the woman she pretended to be.

"What's brought this on, Alex?'' he snapped at her. "Be honest. It has nothing to do with Angelica's claims, does it? You're thinking of yourself. It isn't the fear of having a child that bothers you, it's disappointment that your plans for me won't work.''

She stared at him in shock. "My *plans?*''

He could see right through her now. "You've been trying to tell me something important for days. Circling around it, never quite coming to the point. Now I know what that something is.''

"You do?" She stared up at him, her eyes huge and moist and pleading. But he wouldn't let her off the hook just yet.

"Did you stage that fall from Eros?" he demanded. "Was pretending to injure your shoulder part of the act, or were you just unlucky enough to fall the wrong way and really hurt yourself?"

She stared at him in disbelief. "Stage the fall?" she whispered, her voice hoarse with rage.

"A simple horse trainer from an ordinary middle-class family." He sneered. "Did you decide that wasn't the life for you anymore?"

She drew the tip of her tongue across her lower lip, looking as if she were holding her breath. But she said nothing to deny his accusations.

He didn't care. He'd had it up to *here* with women. He should have stopped there, should have just walked away from her then. But now that he was letting out years of frustrations with the opposite sex, he couldn't seem to separate her from all the others.

"Was I to be your ticket to the rich life?" he bellowed. "If you could trap me into marrying you, just like my ex-wife did, you'd never have to work another day. When did you first target me, Alex? Was it at the royal ball? Or before that?"

She shot a look at him that was as full of fury as he felt. Swerving away from him, she dashed for the stable door. But he was faster. "Let me go!" she shrieked, tears coursing down her cheeks as his fingers closed around her arm. "I wasn't trying to trap you into marriage or anything else! Why would I do that when I'd just run away from one wedding?"

"So you say," he growled.

Her free hand sped in a vicious arc toward the side of

his face, but he intercepted the slap by grabbing her wrist. "I'm glad Angelica filed that suit," he said, "even though her claim is a lie. If she hadn't, I might not have seen through you until it was too late, Alex. It was going to be a damn sight harder to walk away from you as long as I believed you were who you said you were. Now—" a tight smile curled his lips "—now, walking way from you will be easy."

He released her abruptly, whipped around and stalked off across the yard, leaving Alex shaken, her face smudged with tears and dust. She felt as if she'd been beaten to within a breath of her existence, although he'd only restrained her for his own safety. Every nerve in her body felt raw. Her eyes burned and her head throbbed violently.

The worst part of it was, Phillip had gotten the nature of her deception all wrong. He still thought she was who she'd said she was, but she was after his money. She had trapped herself, and now she couldn't win.

If she told him she couldn't care less about his money because she had plenty of her own, he would never speak to her again because she'd lied to him. On the other hand, if she clung to her little hoax and continued to play the role of horse trainer, he would still believe she was the same sort of woman he'd run from all of his life. Women had always wanted something from him. His mother, his wife, this Angelica and all the others in between.

Alex sat down on the ground, her back pressed up against the rough cedar planks of Eros's stall. She dropped her face into her hands, the happiness of blissful days sailing across the blue Mediterranean no more than a memory. Just like Phillip.

He stormed through the villa, straight into his library, the room he'd always found the most relaxing. As soon as the door slammed behind him, Phillip threw himself down on the leather chaise and glared at the ceiling. Why did he even bother with women? Why did he ever dare to hope that one might be any different from the others who had hounded him all of his life?

But this time, it was serious. This time he had nearly let go of his heart. Alex had seemed so fresh and genuine. She had appeared to be selfless and loving. How wrong he'd been. How tragically wrong.

Trying to put her out of his mind, he turned to the other fiasco in his life. Angelica Terro. He wouldn't have remembered her last name if it hadn't been for the legal document Barnaby had brought to him. He only vaguely remembered any details of that fateful weekend. He'd been at an all-time low following the divorce hearing. He'd just needed someone to hold. There was nothing more to it than that.

But whether or not he remembered anything at all about those forty-eight hours, if he had inadvertently fathered a child, he would take that responsibility seriously. It had never crossed his mind to evade his duty. It stung all the more brutally to hear Alex accuse him of not caring, of not doing the right thing.

But he'd promised Barnaby time to feel out the situation, and Phillip would give him that. Then he'd have to make some decisions that might not be easy ones. As it was, he'd already made one of the most difficult of his life. He must stop seeing Alex. He would arrange for her to return to the palace or the States or to go wherever she wished, but she would no longer be welcome at his home or in his bed.

With a supreme effort he shoved himself up off the chaise and poured himself a brandy. Half an hour later, he had notified Cook and his houseman that he would be leaving Altaria for an unspecified number of days. He took everything he'd need with him down to the private dock at the foot of the hill and loaded it onto the smaller of his two yachts, then set sail for wherever the wind took him. By the time he returned, he hoped Alex would be gone.

Alex spent four long days wandering between the villa and the stables, wondering when or if Phillip would ever come back. She had decided after the first day of his absence that she had no choice but to tell him the truth. Things couldn't get any worse, could they?

The second day, she rode Eros in the ring, on the level. No jumps. She talked to the horse, stroked and brushed him, fed him chunks of fresh carrot. That night she wrote about her day's activities in a small leather-bound blank book she'd bought in town. But her imagination took off and soon she was inventing characters and horses that existed only in her mind, and an exciting story began to take shape on paper.

The third day there was still no word from Phillip, and she began to suspect that the staff expected her to leave. But she desperately needed to see Phillip and confess everything to him, so she waited. Again she rode Eros, this time along the beach, kicking up billows of white sand as she stared out at the horizon, watching for the sail of Phillip's boat. In the evening she added to her story of a young woman who was gifted with animals but couldn't make sense of her own life.

On the fourth day, late in the afternoon, Alex saw a tiny blue speck from the beach, and it slowly became a sail that grew larger and larger as it approached the shore, and her heart fluttered with hope. She *knew* it was Phillip!

She returned Eros to his stall, asked a stable boy to unsaddle him and see to his brushing, then she ran down to the dock and sat watching as Phillip dropped first the triangular jib to the bow of the ship, then the larger mainsail, and the yacht glided up against the wooden pilings. He threw a line around one, and secured it, seemingly unaware of her presence.

"Hi, sailor," she murmured softly when he'd come close enough to hear her.

He visibly stiffened, kept his back to her, and said nothing.

"I know you think I'm a terribly shallow, money-grubbing female, but I assure you I'm not after your fortune."

He swung around on her, his eyes dark fires, consuming her. "No? Then what are you after, Alex?" He didn't give her time to answer. "Never mind, I don't want to know."

"It's not fair if you won't even listen to what I have to say," she pleaded.

"It wasn't fair of you to accuse me of being a bad father, when you can't possibly know what I'm thinking or even if I *am* the father."

"I don't suppose it is fair," she whispered. "I was acting on an emotional level."

The tension between them was hot and sharp and nearly unbearable. Alex wished she had left. If she'd just been able to walk away from Phillip, he'd never have known who she really was. But she had to try one last time. She owed him an honest explanation.

"Emotions are something I've tried to live without," he muttered. "Maybe you'd do better to do the same."

She closed her eyes briefly and suffered the pain of his accusations in a silent moment. She supposed she deserved this torture. "Phillip, I—"

"Forget it, Alex. I'm not angry with you anymore. You can think what you like of me. I will do what I believe is right and not ask for your approval. We had a few good days together. Let's leave it at that. I'm sure you have a lot of work to catch up on at the king's stables as well as back home in Chicago.''

He was telling her to leave, that he never wanted to see her again. She dropped her glance to the ground and fought off the terrible sense of rejection. If he didn't want to hear the truth, why bother? It would only add fuel to his argument, only make him think worse of her, if that was possible.

''By the time I pack tonight, it will be too late to show up at the palace with so little warning,'' she whispered. ''I'll leave in the morning, if that's all right with you.''

''Fine,'' he said, turning away from her to coil a dock line.

She stood for a few more minutes, watching him finish with the ropes, then fold the jib into a canvas bag. He was making himself busy, ignoring her. With a bitter taste in her mouth and a weeping heart, she turned back toward the house.

It was after midnight, and Phillip lay in bed. He hadn't been able to rest in one position for more than five minutes. He doubted he'd be able to sleep at all, but tomorrow he'd meet with Barnaby, Angelica and her attorney to come to some sort of agreement, and it promised to be an exhausting day. He needed a clear head to face whatever transpired, but all he could think about was Alex. Tomorrow she would walk out of his life, and he wouldn't stop her.

At last his eyes closed, but his sleep was troubled. He dreamt of a woman with green eyes and pale ivory skin. They stood in his garden, but not a flower bloomed there. She was carrying something in her arms. He walked up to her, feeling an overwhelming burst of anger. He shouted something ugly at the woman, who was clearly Alex, for no one had eyes like hers. Emerald pools. He felt badly for making her cry. He gentled his voice and spoke to her again, but she didn't answer. She looked up at him, and the sorrow in her eyes nearly broke his heart. Slowly, he reached out to peel back the pink blanket that covered whatever she carried.

It was a baby.

The child in her arms began to squall and squirm. He reached out in the dream, took the babe from her arms and rocked it against his chest. He smelled the powder-fresh scent of baby, felt her warm, new life move within his cradling arms, and his heart swelled.

It was *his* baby, his and Alex's. Nothing had ever seemed more precious, more beautiful to him.

Throwing off the covers, Phillip sat up in bed, sweating profusely, shivering when the ocean air through his window hit his damp skin. He raked a hand through his hair and gave it a hard tug, trying to force himself back to reality.

The dream had seemed so very real. Even now, fully awake, he felt an inexplicable loss deep in his gut, as if he'd thrown away a treasure of incalculable value. As if he'd rejected life itself. The life of his progeny.

Striding from the room in only his briefs, he tore down the hallway, found the door behind which Alex slept, opened it and stepped through without knocking.

His breath caught in his throat. She lay on the bed, a pale peach nightgown flowing around her still body. She slept deeply, peacefully, he thought at first—but every now and then she frowned in her sleep and moaned as if in pain. He moved closer to her.

"Alex," he whispered.

She didn't stir.

He stretched out on the bed alongside her and gently touched a wisp of ebony hair trailing across her eyelid. Moving it aside, he kissed her feathery, dark lashes then lifted her arm away from her body. Phillip slid himself closer to her and felt the warmth of her body against his chest, his thighs.

He kissed her cheek. Kissed the tip of her nose. Kissed her sleep-warm lips and lingered there, savoring their sweetness. Her eyes drifted open but she didn't pull away.

Slowly, the initial tension in her body of realizing she wasn't alone, melted away. "What are you doing?" she whispered between his parted lips.

"I'm saying I'm sorry for treating you so badly when you were just being honest with me. You told me how you felt about men who ran out on their children. I shouldn't have taken it personally. I should have just told you what was going on."

"About the honesty part," she began, "I have something to tell you, and it can't wait."

He shook his head. "There's too much happening right now, Alex. Let me deal with this lawsuit first. I don't want you to become tangled up in that mess. After I've straightened that out, we can talk all you want about us. If you want there to be an *us.*"

"I do," she said, tears clinging like liquid jewels to her fine lashes. "I do want to find a way to—"

"Hush," he said, covering her lips with his.

This time he was prepared. Before leaving his own bedroom he'd hastily foraged in his night table and found the protection he'd left there. Now he quickly slid off his briefs and, as Alex watched him with wide, gleaming eyes, he smoothed the latex over his full erection.

He burned for her. He needed her as he'd needed no

other woman in his life. And if his dream had any truth to it, this simple young woman who had lived half her life in stables would become an even more important part of his life.

He moved over her body and smiled down at her. "Why look so apprehensive, Alex? I said I'm sorry." He ran a hand inside her nightdress, stroking upward along her silky thigh, to her hip, the flat of her stomach then found her breast. The nipple hardened and peaked between his thumb and forefinger. He rubbed it until he felt her go limp beneath him. "Let's make love now. Let's not think about tomorrow or any other day."

Her arms came up around his neck and she gave him a weak smile. "All right," she said. "Make me remember tonight forever." Her voice held a finality he didn't understand. But his desire for her was so strong he didn't ask what she meant. Now was not a time for talk.

Phillip slid his hands beneath her hips to raise and angle them just slightly toward him. Moving his own hips below hers, he thrust himself forward and up. She opened herself to him at just the right moment, and wrapped her long legs around his waist. He drove himself into her hot, moist center. Arching her back, she met him with equal passion, and together they reached heights he'd never believed possible.

Alex woke only once during the night. She lay in Phillip's arms and wished it could be like this forever. Even then she knew that was impossible.

He believed they had made up and everything was all right. But she knew better. Although he'd reassured her that he would do the right thing for Angelica, or for any other woman who had his baby, if it should come to that, she still hadn't told him the truth about herself. Time was running out. If he went to the reception at the palace next weekend, someone there was bound to give her away. Someone would tell him that she was a Connelly, the sister of the new king, not an employee.

Time was running very short indeed.

Nine

Phillip lay only half-awake. He waited until Alex stirred against his body. Neither had bothered putting on anything to sleep in, and a cool breeze blew off the Mediterranean, freshening the room and everything in it. From the angle of the sun, he supposed it might be nearly ten o'clock. He hadn't slept so blissfully, so deeply in a very long time.

He touched Alex's shoulder, wondering how long she would stay with him. Part of him wanted that to be forever, but another part still fought permanency. He'd learned the hard way that the price for commitment could be harsh. He never wanted to make that mistake again. But Alex… wasn't she different? She might have secrets, but he would earn her trust and wean them from her.

"I'm awake," she whispered. "Kiss me."

"Yes, m'lady," he said and did so.

Her lips tasted like honey. Her breath was sweet and her body ripe. He would have liked to make love to her again, but there had been a reason he'd returned to Altaria when he did.

"I have to get up," he said regretfully. "The hearing is today." He felt her body tense, then she turned her head to one side and those green eyes that had captured his heart from the moment he'd first seen them gazed up at him with concern.

"What will happen, Phillip? I mean, I know you think it's impossible. But if it turns out that you are the father, will you—" She hesitated.

"If you're trying to say, will I marry Angelica, forget it. I doubt that's what she wants anyway. Barnaby seems to think she's after a quick, out-of-court settlement. A fat onetime handout. But I'm not sure."

Alex frowned. "Then what's your theory?"

"It's my guess there's more to this that we know at this point. Barnaby's already mentioned the danger of Angelica coming back, holding the child's welfare over me to demand more money, over and over again."

"That's almost as bad as blackmail."

"It's extortion of a sort, true." He smoothed one wide hand down the side of Alex's body, over her hip and outer thigh. She felt like warm satin, and he loved lingering in her bed like this.

"So what will you do?"

"Go and hear what she and her lawyer have to say. Listen carefully, and try to do what's right. I won't lie and say I've never seen the woman before, even though that might be the wisest move. I've never lied in my life and can't abide people who do." He thought he saw her wince. "What's wrong, Alex?"

"Nothing," she said. "I'm just worried…that you'll still end up being caught up in her scam."

He laughed and pulled her out from beneath the sheets

and into his arms. Her fingertips curled against his bare chest and laced through the wiry dark curls. She was warm and caring and marvelous. "I would like you to come with me this morning."

She turned in his arms to look up at him. "Why?"

"I'm not sure. Perhaps another set of ears to hear the woman's story and tell me if it rings true. You seem to be a good judge of character—horses' and people's. Having another woman's viewpoint represented might be a good thing, too."

"All right," she agreed, but he sensed reluctance in her tone. He didn't ask why. There wasn't time for lengthy discussion. They were supposed to be at the lawyer's office at noon.

Phillip let her down gently onto the bed. "I'll go shower and leave you to get ready. We should head for town in an hour. I promised Barnaby we'd meet him twenty minutes early in case he had any more information by then."

Alex nodded, then watched Phillip as he left her room. A confusing mix of emotions struggled against each other within her. She had been overjoyed when he came to her the night before. But she knew in her heart that his return changed nothing. A lie stood between them as immovable as a stone wall, and it was clearer to her than ever that revealing the truth to him would make him trust her less, not more.

What was she to do? She didn't have a clue.

Alex took a long, very hot shower, putting off the moment when she must step out of the soothing rush of water and face the day. Phillip was in no state of mind to hear her confession on the way to the hearing. Yet, if she waited even another hour, wasn't she just avoiding the inevitable? Her stomach felt as if it had tied itself in one huge knot.

Without giving her outfit much thought, she dressed in the only suit she'd brought on the trip—a simple tan linen with a short skirt—and conservative heels. It had been the outfit she had intended to wear away from her wedding reception when she left on her honeymoon with Robert.

How long ago that day seemed. It almost seemed part of another woman's life, certainly not hers. She was glad she had left her fiancé, glad she had found Phillip. It was strange how things sometimes worked out when you least expected them to. Perhaps, with a great deal of luck, it would be that way for her when she finally told Phillip who she was. She could always hope.

Alex stepped out onto the purple wisteria-shaded veranda of the villa and looked out over the distant water. The Mediterranean called to her. She remembered their weekend of adventure. Free of money. Free of all cares. It had seemed so perfect.

Strange. She had never felt so alive as during those two days. Life had never seemed so real, or so full of promise.

"There's time for a quick breakfast, if you like." Phillip was seated at a white wicker table spread with pastries and a carafe of coffee. But her stomach soured at the mention of food.

"Nothing for me, thanks," she murmured.

Phillip stood and walked over to her. He looked down at her. "Then I guess we should go. Are you ready?"

"If you are." An unfamiliar noise caught Alex's attention. She turned toward the stables. Shouts and three loud bangs that sounded like something hard whacking against wood came from that direction. "Do you hear that?"

Phillip scowled and cocked his head as if to listen better. "Could be the stable lads are having trouble with one of the horses."

The shouts grew more strident, frantic. Alex couldn't

imagine what was going on. She moved forward and gripped the veranda's rail with both hands. "It sounds as if it's coming from the stalls at this end."

"Yes." Phillip was already moving down the steps.

"That's where Eros is stabled!" she called after him.

He didn't answer but broke into a run. Alex took off after him as fast as her dress pumps allowed. Her heart thudded in her chest. Her mouth had gone dry. *Eros!*

Please don't let anything happen to him! she thought frantically. She'd grown to love the horse, she now realized, almost as much as she loved his master.

By the time they reached the long, white barn, an explosion of yells, crashes and curses met them. From inside the dark interior, Alex glimpsed a flash of lustrous black then heard the unmistakable heaving of a horse's frightened breathing. Hooves pounded in rapid syncopation against packed dirt. Alex looked to her right. Eros's stall was empty The horse was running wild.

"Eros is loose!" she shouted at Phillip.

He swore under his breath and dashed inside the stable. Alex raced after him.

"Where is he?" Phillip shouted at one of the younger stable boys, who appeared to be running away from instead of toward the commotion.

"Round the other aisle now, sir. He broke out while we was cleanin' his stall. Sorry, we didn't—"

"Never mind that now!" Phillip snapped. "Throw me that rope and bridle!"

Alex stood for a moment, hands braced on her knees as she tried to catch her breath. But Phillip was off and running again, disappearing between two stalls. She ran to catch up with him.

She might not be the experienced trainer she'd pretended to be, but Alex sensed that the panicky shouts fill-

ing the stable weren't going to help Phillip's staff calm or
capture a frightened horse. Eros was too strong, too fast
and easily capable of doing damage to people or property
while he was caught up in fear.

She hesitated only a second before running for the tack
room. Kicking off her dress shoes and ripping off panty
hose, she reached for her riding boots. There was no time
to change into breeches. She grabbed a crop and rushed
back into the straw-covered alley that ran the length of the
stable. No one was in sight, and all sounds indicated the
action had moved to the far side of the yard.

Once outside, she could see a line of young men waving
their arms over their heads and screaming, "Alt! Alt!"

She caught a glimpse of Phillip trying to herd the huge
black gelding toward them, obviously hoping the human
fence would contain the animal. If cornered, Phillip must
have thought, the horse might then be captured.

Alex knew better. She'd ridden and been thrown by
Eros, and she'd ridden him since then and learned the trig-
gers that set him off. She'd learned too the small ways he
could be comforted. Someone was sure to be hurt, for although the horse had a big, loving heart, terror would blind
him. He wouldn't stop for a few people standing in his
way.

"Get out of his way!" she shouted. "He'll run right
over you. He's too scared to stop!"

Two of the men glanced in her direction, confusion mir-
rored in their expressions. Eros wheeled, then reared high,
his front hooves slicing the air as he let out a frantic
whinny that sounded like a distress call. His hooves hit the
dirt. He dug in, then began his charge for freedom.

"Look out!" she screamed.

The line of men broke, and Eros shot between them. He

turned toward the road, his muzzle frothing, eyes rolled back in alarm.

Phillip glared at her across the yard. "Why the hell did you do that?"

"He would have trampled them!"

She sensed he understood. But the problem of a loose, dangerous animal remained. Phillip looked at her. "We have to stop him before he reaches the highway or town."

He was right. She had thought only of the immediate situation, which had been bad enough.

"We'll take the Jeep!" Phillip shouted to one of his men. "See if we can head him off before town." He shot her a warning glare. "Stay here, Alex."

Feeling helpless, she stood by as he jumped into the vehicle, took the wheel, then sped off in a cloud of dust. Sorry, Phillip, she thought, I can't do that. She couldn't just sit still while Eros was in danger or put others in jeopardy. What good was a Jeep going to do anyway? It couldn't go where a runaway horse could go.

She ran back into the stable, straight to the mare whose stall was next to Eros's. As stablemates, they were chums. Lucy's presence might calm the other horse, might help her coax him into remembering that he needn't fear the woman who had ridden him for the past several days.

Quickly, Alex saddled Lucy and mounted her. She grabbed a spare halter from a nail in the wall as they passed by. She galloped out of the yard and turned toward the steep path that led through the woods, down from the villa directly toward town. With any luck, Eros would have slowed some after leaving the shouting, hand-waving mob behind. And her route was shorter, as she would cut across the road the horse had taken before he hit the highway or town.

Alex leaned back in the saddle and let the mare negotiate the precipitous dirt trail. Lucy was accustomed to the trail and plunged down it with sure footing. As soon as they were on flat ground, Alex kicked her into a gallop.

In the distance, she could hear the whine of an engine. The Jeep! Phillip had taken the same road as Eros. A mistake, she feared, because the noise of the vehicle would drive the horse away all the faster.

At the junction of the trail with the main road, Alex brought the mare to a stop and stood in the stirrups, waiting, gulping down air, straining to hear the telltale sound of hoofbeats above the pounding of her own heart. Was she too late?

Then, suddenly, a horse's hooves clattered furiously along the pavement of the road just above her. Eros. He was coming this way. The mare danced nervously, sensing the other horse's panic, but Alex steadied her and whispered in her ear. "It's okay, Lucy. Just your old pal come to visit."

At the far end of the curve in the road, the immense black equine at last appeared, as wild-eyed and fierce-looking as any Saracen mount. He was moving fast, ebony mane and tail flying out behind him. Alex checked for traffic coming the other way. Luckily there was none.

She slowly walked Lucy into the center of the road so that Eros would be sure to see them. Forcing herself to sit erect in the saddle and appear calm, Alex waited.

Eros didn't break stride, but he tossed his head as if curious about the horse and rider before him. He could have darted around them if he wished; nothing blocked his way. Although he must have been tired by then, if he sensed any aggressiveness from Alex, she knew he'd surely take off again.

But she was doing nothing to alarm him. And she was

betting that the exhausted horse's social instincts and need for the familiar would outweigh his desire to run.

Halfway to her, Eros shifted to a skitterish canter, then slowed to a lazy amble. He danced to one side, spun once, looked her and Lucy over, then circled around them. His huge chest heaving from exertion, he timidly approached them and, at last, nuzzled Lucy's neck with frothy lips.

"Hey there, boy," Alex said in the same calm tone she'd greeted him in the stables every day.

She could hear the metallic whine of the Jeep growing louder, and she prayed it wouldn't come around the bend until she'd gotten the horses off the road.

"Good, Eros. Nice boy. Want to go for a walk now? How about some nice oats back home, huh?" Slowly, ever so slowly, she dropped the halter she'd brought with her over his ears. They ticked once, but he was too happy to see Lucy to pull away.

Alex's fingers worked quickly as she continued speaking in a low, soothing voice. A moment later, she'd secured the chin strap and held the reins. Still riding Lucy, she walked the two horses to the side of the road and waited.

The Jeep whipped around the bend and rushed past them as Alex casually lifted a hand to wave. Brakes screeched. The vehicle stopped in the middle of the road, then slowly began to back up.

The look of astonishment on Phillip's face was deliciously gratifying. "Well, I'll be—" He let out a long breath. "The three of you are one beautiful sight." He squinted at Alex's skirt. "Looks like you split something."

"I didn't exactly have time to change." She glanced down at the beige gabardine, hiked up nearly to her waist to accommodate her legs straddling the saddle. One side seam had opened up, exposing the length of her bare leg to the hip. Dirt kicked up by Lucy's hooves spattered her skin. "Guess I'll need another shower."

Phillip looked at the man in the seat beside him, who just shook his head in amazement. But when Phillip turned back to her, his expression grew serious. "You're an amazing woman, Alex. You could have been hurt. It wouldn't be an exaggeration to say you'd risked your life for that horse."

"But I'm fine," she said.

"What about Eros?"

"He seems to be all right now. I think he just found himself out of the stall and would have eventually wandered back in for his feed if everyone hadn't become hysterical. They scared him, and once he was running he stopped thinking."

"Sometimes that happens," he said. His eyes locked with hers and conveyed a clear message. "We run from our ghosts, even though it's often the worst thing to do."

She knew what he meant. She'd been running a long time from life. Phillip had been running, too—from women who used him, from women who lied. As soon as the hearing was over, she vowed she would tell him everything. She wouldn't be one of those women.

Phillip followed Barnaby into the other lawyer's office. Alex walked silently beside him. He felt her presence as an unexpected comfort. Her support and belief in him made a difficult situation bearable.

Yet he sensed how traumatic the meeting might be for Alex. It didn't matter that his association with Angelica Terro had been fleeting and without emotional attachment. He would have felt just as uneasy standing in a room with Alex's former fiancé.

He turned his attention to the delicate problem at hand.

The windowless gray conference room they were led to felt so hot it was difficult to breathe. Even though Phillip knew he was in the right, the muscles in his shoulders and neck tightened to steel bands. A trickle of sweat rolled down his back between his shoulder blades, and the fresh dress shirt he'd hastily pulled on after returning Eros to his stall stuck to his spine.

He told himself he wanted to do the right thing. But what that might be depended upon Angelica. Was she trying to con him? Or did she honestly believe he was the father of her child? If so, she was asking of him no more than she had a right.

He looked across the cramped, airless room at the olive-complected woman already seated to one side of the single desk. She glanced quickly up at him, then down again at the sleeping baby in her arms. The child appeared to be no more than nine months old, but could have been as young as seven months or as old as a year, which would have meant she was already pregnant at the time of his assignation with her.

He tried to catch Angelica's eyes to better read her, but she persisted in avoiding his gaze.

"Have a seat, please," the lawyer said with forced politeness. He introduced himself as Raphael Giovini and proceeded to read his client's statement, which indicated that Phillip alone could have been the baby's father.

Phillip listened without comment until the man had finished. Barnaby slanted a look at him then started to speak. But Phillip put out a hand, silencing him. "May I speak to Angelica in private?"

"No," Giovini said sharply. "She is too afraid that you will harm her or the child."

Phillip shot Alex a distressed look. He'd never hurt another human being in his life. It was ridiculous to think he would now, under these circumstances. The warm glow in Alex's eyes let him know she believed in him.

"All right," Phillip said, "we'll do it your way. But let's keep this as simple as possible. Yes, I was intimate with this woman, and it might have been about the time she conceived this child."

Giovini smiled. "I'm glad you are being reasonable, sir."

"I want to take a DNA test and bring that evidence before a court for a formal hearing."

The lawyer looked taken aback and glanced at Angelica. Her eyes widened, and she moved her head from side to side so subtly the signal was almost unnoticeable.

Giovini coughed delicately into one hand. "We had supposed, Prince Phillip, that you would prefer to handle this quietly, out of the public eye. Your recent divorce caused you much painful scandal. We wouldn't want to put you or your mother in that position again."

"I'm sure not," Phillip stated, keeping his growing annoyance with the man in check. "But more than my privacy is at stake here. This is a matter of honor, sir. I want to take the test."

"Phillip," Barnaby cautioned, resting a hand on his arm, "remember what I said. And the paparazzi, as you know, can be ruthless."

Phillip brushed him off. "If the DNA doesn't match, then I'm not the father. If we go to court, I want everyone to see those results."

"Everyone?" A glint surfaced in Giovini's shrewd eyes. "I'm sure your mother would much prefer—"

"My mother," Phillip snapped, "has nothing to do with this situation! I don't care one way or the other what she thinks about it." It wasn't the absolute truth; she could make his life a living hell if she felt inconvenienced or embarrassed by his social life. But he didn't have to tell the lawyer that.

He turned to Angelica. "It's up to you. Do you wish to pursue this further?"

She looked far less at ease than when he'd first entered the room.

Phillip continued. "Perhaps your lawyer hasn't properly explained to you the penalty for falsely accusing a man of fathering your child. You could end up in jail, you realize. Extortion is a serious offense."

Angelica shot to her feet, her baby clutched to her chest. She was shouting at Giovini in an excited muddle of Italian and the island patois. Alex could make out almost none of what she was saying, but it was clear that the woman didn't like the new odds.

The lawyer spoke quickly and firmly in Italian, trying to calm her down, but she only shook her head angrily at him. She switched to English, as if she wanted everyone in the room to understand her. "I'm leaving, Raphael. It's no good."

"Sit down!" he shouted at her. "He's bluffing. He doesn't want—"

"Don't speak for me!" Phillip growled furiously. "I think it would be best if both of you gentlemen left the room and let me speak with this young woman."

Alex stood by, holding her breath. She sensed that Phillip was taking a terrible risk but she understood, too, that his good name was precious to him. He would do whatever he must to protect his honor.

Barnaby gestured with an open hand toward the door, and Giovini shot Phillip a venomous glare but left the office, followed by Barnaby. The door shut behind the two lawyers. The room was deathly silent for a moment.

Alex stood up from her chair. "I should go, too," she whispered.

"No, stay." Phillip's voice remained tight yet controlled, as if he was aware he must not frighten Angelica any further or she would bolt. "I'll need a witness in the room in case Ms. Terro should claim I assaulted or threatened her."

Alex met the other woman's eyes, and saw that he was right. A shadow of cleverness darkened her gaze. Alex sat down again to listen.

Phillip turned to Angelica. "Who talked you into this?"

The woman settled herself in her chair and sullenly fingered the blanket around her sleeping baby. She admitted nothing, but her eyes grew moist and worried.

"I know that you wouldn't have agreed to this scam unless you were desperate. Am I right?" Phillip asked, his voice gentler still.

She said nothing, but tears started to fall down her cheeks.

"Was it that sly fox of a lawyer?" Phillip asked. "I assure you, he's misled you if he's promised you'll walk out of here with a carload of money and no fight from me."

"My boyfriend," Angelica whimpered. "He thought... he *said*, if you are so rich and we are so poor, why would you miss a few thousand dollars?"

"But once the lawyer got involved, he upped the ante, is that right?"

She nodded. "He promised us much wealth." Her gaze shot to Alex, then back to Phillip. "I don't want to go to jail. What would become of my baby? *He* won't take care of it."

"You won't go to jail," Phillip assured her. "Just drop the suit."

Alex stood and went over to the woman, feeling suddenly sorry for her. She rested a hand on her shoulder. "Your boyfriend, is he the father?"

Angelica nodded. "I don't know what I'll do. I cannot work and take care of the baby properly. My family, they all live in the north, in Milano. They won't have me there. And my man, he has no job."

Alex looked to Phillip. His eyes closed for a moment, as if he was thinking very hard.

"If you would sign a document," he said at last, "freeing me of all responsibility for the child, I will help you."

"Help how?" Angelica asked, sniffling as she rocked the sleeping child.

Alex listened as Phillip outlined an immediate cash gift to buy the baby clothes and food. He also promised to pay the rent for a small apartment until Angelica could find work in her home that wouldn't take her from the baby.

Looking relieved, Angelica reached across the desk and grabbed paper and a pen. She wrote a few sentences and signed the statement. Phillip wrote out a check and handed it to her, pledging another check as soon as she located a decent apartment on the island. She left, looking far happier than before, and Phillip turned to Alex.

"I'm going to ask Barnaby about setting up a small trust for the baby. I feel I should do something. Even though that clearly isn't my child, it could have been."

Alex put her arms around him and kissed him. "Thank you."

"I didn't do anything for you," he said, sounding surprised.

"Oh yes, you did," she murmured. "You've proven the kind of man you are." She gazed up at him adoringly. Was it love or just admiration for a remarkable, generous man? Maybe a little of both.

It was late afternoon by the time they returned to the villa. The stables had been restored to their customary peace, and Alex sensed that Phillip's mind was now at ease. As she walked into the blissfully cool interior of the stucco mansion, she wished she felt as much confidence in their relationship.

"You look tired," Phillip said as she paused in the foyer and looked around, aware that her days in this beautiful place might be numbered.

"I am, I guess," she admitted. "First chasing down Eros, then…"

She didn't need to explain; he seemed to understand. "Thank you for being there with me," he said. "It must have been difficult for you."

"It was, in a way," she admitted. "But I was glad it all worked out so well. You were more than fair with her."

Phillip kissed her on the tip of her nose. "There's time to rest up before dinner. Why don't you take a nap? I have to call Barnaby and finish some paperwork, then I'll join you on the veranda."

She nodded, although she was sure sleep would be impossible. There was too much on her mind.

In her room, Alex practiced the words she'd use to finally tell Phillip who she really was. The risk was great. She prayed he'd offer her the same generosity and understanding he'd given Angelica Terro.

Ten

That evening Cook prepared a meal that leaned suspiciously toward the romantic, and Phillip wondered if the woman was trying to aid and abet his own feelings. He wanted to be close to Alex that night, closer than ever before. He knew something important was on her mind, and he aimed to make sharing that with him easy for her. He wanted her to continue trusting him as she had earlier.

She had stood by him twice that day. Saving him from possible disaster when Eros broke free, then supporting him through the distressing meeting at a crooked lawyer's office. The first situation could have ended very badly, with loss of life and property. And without her in Giovini's office, he might not have been able to settle the matter with Angelica in a manner that not only helped the troubled young woman but also preserved his reputation.

He smiled at Alex when she crossed the veranda and took the crystal stem of champagne from him. But he could tell she was nervous again. Her green eyes swept across his gardens, brilliant with tropical blossoms, avoiding him. As he stood silently waiting for her to speak, the tension between them grew.

He had no idea where it came from, this negative force that pricked at him, so that as soon as he felt drawn to Alex, he sensed her pushing him away. Even as they'd made love earlier, there was that mysterious struggle between them. They were like the ends of two magnets. When turned one way they drew together with amazing force; when one was turned the other way around, the energy repelled just as strongly.

Cook served their meal. Phillip picked at the lobster tail swimming in melted butter on his plate. He watched Alex take a long sip of her champagne, then put the delicate crystal stemware down with shaking fingers. What was so difficult for her to say to him? Perhaps he could encourage her by starting the conversation.

"I can't tell you," he began, "how much I appreciate all you did today."

She looked across the table at him, her right eyebrow lifting. "Me? I didn't do anything special," she murmured quickly, as if embarrassed at the thought.

"Come on now," he said with a forced laugh. "Eros might have been killed if he'd reached the highway before we caught him. Or, as you yourself pointed out, he might have trampled someone in his state of panic. You risked your life to go after him the way you did."

"I suppose," she murmured, her sad gaze returning to her untouched plate.

He reached out a hand and rested it over hers on the tablecloth. "What's wrong, Alex? You can tell me. Does it still have something to do with Angelica?"

She shook her head. "No. I was very proud of you. You

knew from the beginning that you weren't the father of that child, yet you were so willing to help them. Because of you, they have a chance of making it.'' She smiled sweetly at him, but behind the smile something dark loomed.

He took a deep breath. ''So now you know,'' he said slowly, with emphasis, to make sure she understood, ''that I'd never desert you if you needed me.''

She looked stricken.

''That's a good thing, isn't it?'' He frowned, sensing her unwillingness, even now, to speak words that were painful to her. ''Unless you aren't interested in continuing our relationship. Is that it?''

He looked away from her when she didn't answer, picked up his glass and drank down the remainder of his champagne in a single swallow. His stomach clenched and his hand felt unsteady as he placed the flute back on the table.

Perhaps he'd been too confident all along. She wasn't worried about his staying with her, after all. She was trying to think of a gentle way to tell him goodbye. What an idiot he'd been.

''No,'' she whispered at last. ''Of course that's not it.'' She turned her hand over and laced her fingers with his, holding him as if she wanted to prevent his pulling away from her. ''You see, when we first met—''

''What is it?'' Phillip demanded impatiently.

She stopped midsentence, at first not realizing that he was speaking to someone else. Following his stony glare, she turned to find one of his servants standing behind her chair.

''Miss has a telephone call,'' the man said. ''A Mr. Grant Connelly from the United States. Shall I bring the phone here or—''

"I'll take it inside," Alex said quickly.

"I hope your employer isn't summoning you home," Phillip said.

Alex shot him a strange look he couldn't interpret then rushed from the table.

He poured himself more champagne, wishing for something stronger. His nerves stung with anticipation. He wished to God that he could read Alex's mind. It couldn't be as bad as she was making it out to be. Could it?

Maybe the Connellys were putting pressure on her to leave, to return to her job back in Chicago. He could fix that. He could offer her a higher salary to come to Altaria and work for him. He'd make sure her hours were short, so that they'd have plenty of time to spend together.

Whatever was wrong, he was sure he could handle it…if she let him. If she wasn't just looking for a way out.

In the dim foyer, Alex picked up the phone. She had been so close to telling Phillip everything. So very close. She was out of breath, dizzy and disoriented. If it hadn't been for her father's call, she would have blurted out her whole story right then and there.

But she couldn't put her father off when so much was happening within the family. They had all been terribly frightened when Daniel had come so close to death, and now that they were sure it had been an intentional attempt on his life and the investigation might turn up valuable evidence at any moment, she knew she had to talk to Grant.

"Hi, Daddy, what's up?" she asked in a whisper, hoping none of the staff was near enough to hear her. She stepped to one side, bringing the phone with her so that she could see Phillip sitting on the veranda.

"I wanted to update you on the investigation from this

side of the pond," he said, using the English way of referring to the Atlantic. "I told you I was having Charlotte followed?"

"Yes?"

"Well, it seems she was acting strange for a reason. They tracked her to an obstetrician's office. She's pregnant."

Alex nearly laughed with relief. "Well, that's innocent enough. What woman wouldn't be acting odd if she thought she might be pregnant? She's not married, right?"

"No."

"Well, there you go." Alex couldn't wait to get off the phone, now that she knew the news wasn't serious. Phillip looked restless. "She has a dilemma, and it's been preying on her mind."

Alex could almost see Grant shaking his head in his grim way, as if he were in a board meeting, shooting down a proposal from one of his junior execs. "It may well be more than that. She's not making public the identity of the father. And that might have some bearing on the case."

"How?"

"If she's in trouble, she could be vulnerable to certain situations. Let's say that someone has infiltrated the company and is working against the family, then this person could be blackmailing her, threatening to reveal information that might cost her job. She might be protecting the father of her child, or, if he's conspiring against us, she might be feeding him information. We just don't know, but she could be the weak link in the organization."

"But she seems so nice," Alex said with a sigh.

"We're playing with unscrupulous people, my dear. Don't forget that. They're capable of killing to get what they want, so they're capable of anything. Starwind and Reynolds know that, and you should, too."

She closed her eyes, suddenly feeling very cold. She trembled. "I guess you're right." It was just that here, with Phillip, she had felt safe. Murder and treachery seemed so distant, even though it was here, in Altaria, where it had all begun.

"So when are you coming home?" Grant asked. "Your mother and I are worried about you."

"I know you are. I'm so sorry you and Mom were left to explain your daughter's disappearance. We'll talk more when I come home. Let's just say, for now, that I had my reasons for rushing off the way I did."

"I've never doubted that," Grant said firmly. "And if you ever want to confide in us, you know that your mother and I are here for you, Alexandra."

"Thank you, Daddy."

It seemed to Alex a shame that now, when things were suddenly becoming clear to her, when she was finally grasping what life was all about, finally understanding how happy she could be with the very simplest of lives, she might lose it all by admitting to the man who meant the world to her that she had deceived him.

Five minutes later, she hung up the phone. Her head felt so full at the moment. Her brother's upcoming coronation, an attempt on his life, the possibility of her father's company being the target of industrial espionage, the mysterious person following her. She should be home, helping her family through these trying times.

Yet her heart was here in Altaria, and she owed Phillip the truth. Now. No more stalling, no more interruptions.

Alex turned to leave the foyer when she glimpsed a flash of something light-colored on the landing above her. She looked up the stairway toward her room, barely visible around the corner. She was certain she heard a door open.

A thread of light passed across the dim hallway. A latch clicked shut.

Alex frowned. It could have been a maid of course. But her room was usually cleaned early in the day. Her shoulder ached dully, as if reacting to a change in the weather, or a warning of some sort.

Rubbing the sore joint thoughtfully, Alex crossed the foyer and climbed the stairs to the second floor. As she neared the top, she thought about her father's warning. A voice at the very back of her mind told her she should call Phillip or have one of the staff go with her, just in case there really was an intruder. Another voice reminded her how foolish she'd feel if she'd been spooked by one of the maids.

Slowly, she stepped onto the lush silk oriental carpet that lined the hallway. For a moment she stood there, not moving, just listening. Muffled footfalls came from inside one of the rooms, moving cautiously, as if not wanting to be heard. Were they coming from her room? She turned her back on her room to look down the long passageway dimly lit by antique sconces. All of the other doors were closed, too.

There was a click behind her, and she spun around to find Gregor Paulus, his hand still on her doorknob. He looked as startled as she felt, his lips quivering, then he produced a wary smile.

"There you are, miss. I've been looking for you."

"In my room?" She narrowed her eyes at him suspiciously. "Maria didn't tell me you were here."

"I couldn't find her," he said, as quick as ever with his answers. "So I thought I'd not bother the staff. I have an important message from your brother."

"He could have telephoned," she said tightly. She

didn't believe the man. She was certain he'd been snooping through her room.

"I'm sorry if I've intruded," Paulus said obsequiously. "I was only trying to be discreet. You see, I know what you've been doing."

The words settled like an icy blanket of snow over a sunny day. Was the man threatening her? "I don't understand," she said slowly.

"Your little game with the prince of Silverdorn." His smile turned sly and humorless, reptilian. "He doesn't know who you are, does he, Ms. Connelly? You've convinced him you're a common working girl, isn't that so?"

She took a step back, her insides taut. "My relationship with Phillip Kinrowan is none of your business. You're supposed to be my brother's aide. That duty doesn't include spying on his sister." She was furious, and it showed in her tone. Her voice was louder than was wise, but she was losing her patience with the man.

"I'm only looking out for our young king's best interests," Paulus objected smoothly. He appeared entirely too pleased with himself.

"I don't think you are, sir," Alex hissed. "I think you might be looking out for your own interests, whatever they may be. Maybe I should tell Daniel that you've been stalking me, and see what he thinks of that."

She hadn't known for sure that it had been Paulus, but as soon as she'd accused him, his face paled. Her guess had apparently been on target.

"I'm offended!" Paulus snapped. "Why would I follow you around when I have—"

"What's going on up there?" a voice roared from the foyer below.

Alex spun around to see Phillip rushing up the stairs in

twos. Her heart jammed itself up into her throat. How much had he heard?

Above all, she couldn't allow him to learn of her deception from someone else. *She* must be the one to tell him. She kicked herself for having waited so long.

Gregor Paulus snapped to attention, his beady eyes gleaming. "I've come with a message from the king for—"

"For me," Alex said hastily. "I'm going to have to go over to the palace for a few hours tomorrow. Gregor," she said, turning to the royal aide, "thank you for stopping by to tell me on your way into town. I appreciate it. I'll speak with you about this tomorrow." She made sure he understood from her expression that she wouldn't tell Phillip he'd been snooping through her room if he didn't let the cat out of the bag for her.

Paulus executed a stiff bow. "I'll look forward to seeing you," he said, his expression devoid of all its former sinister gleam. Had she imagined it before? He turned toward the stairs.

Phillip waited until he heard the front door open then close with a solid clack. He turned to Alex. "What was that all about?"

She started to move toward the stairs. "Let's finish dinner. I'm still hungry."

"Alex, we need to talk. You've been trying to tell me something for days, and I've put you off. Now that slimy aide-de-camp shows up, and neither of you look as if you're telling the truth."

She was already halfway down the stairs to the foyer, and he had no option but to follow her out onto the veranda. She sat down at the table, sipped from her glass of champagne, and her gaze took in the breadth of the horizon. It was the look of a woman who wasn't going to stay in one place for much longer, and his heart lurched desperately.

"If I were to tell you," she whispered with effort, "that you didn't really know me, that we may have moved too quickly to give a long-lasting relationship a chance at—"

"I'd think you were trying to dump me," he said with a laugh. Almost immediately, his face straightened. "We started this same conversation once before. What are you trying to say, Alex?" He hesitated when she dropped her head forward and stared hopelessly into her hands in her lap. "Are you trying to say you're leaving, Alex?"

She shook her head, looking tormented. "No. No, that's not what I'm trying to do. I just think that…well, sometimes first impressions…they aren't always accurate. Are they?"

He scowled, totally confused now. What on earth was the woman getting at? "You mean, I've misunderstood something about you? Then straighten me out. What should I know about you that's different?"

Her words caught in her throat, giving them a raspy edge. "Just about everything." Alex's thin arms wrapped protectively around her ribs. Her lovely face paled to the shade of the marble statues in his garden.

Phillip stared at her, feeling suddenly very cold. "You don't work for the Connelly family, do you?"

"No."

A rage had started to build on the hurt that came with the knowledge she'd lied to him. Lied to him not just once, but for days, and in the most intimate of situations. "Then why were you at the ball the night we met? Why did you seem so close to them when I first saw you that night?"

She let out a deep sigh. "Because…because…" She bit down on her bottom lip so hard he was sure in another instant she'd draw blood.

"Because you're one of them. You're a Connelly," he guessed, and the moment he'd said it, he could see from the shattered look in her eyes that he was right.

Phillip fell back into his chair and glared at her. She had deliberately deceived him. She'd played him for a fool. How she must have laughed when he'd confided in her about his marriage, about fearing women who were after his money and title! Had she boasted to her brother, the new king, about her little game?

"The only time you were honest with me was when you told me you liked to playact at being someone else. You were pretending to be a horse trainer that night."

"Yes." The single word sounded as if it had been ripped from her.

"You even came here to my home in the hope of convincing me you could retrain Eros. And you kept up the deception for weeks."

"Yes," she admitted again. Tears streamed down her soft cheeks, but he felt not an ounce of pity for her. "Yes…yes," she sobbed.

"Is that all you can say, Alex?" he roared, pushing out of his chair to his feet.

He took two long steps around the table and spun her chair around. Bracing clenched fists on the wicker arms, he leaned over her and spoke into her face. "What is it you want from me, woman?"

"Nothing, nothing!" She wept uncontrollably. "I never wanted anything from you, Phillip. I swear there was no such motive. I just got caught up in the fantasy. By the time I realized what a horrible thing I'd done, by the time it really counted…it was too late to tell you. I was afraid of—" She broke off and stared at him as if terrified of continuing.

He fought the desire to comfort her. She didn't deserve

his compassion, he told himself. Not after what she'd done to him, not after the way she'd so selfishly toyed with his emotions.

"Afraid of what?" he growled.

"Afraid of losing you." The words slipped between her lips so softly he wasn't absolutely sure he'd heard them.

But words no longer mattered, not when they came from a woman whose rich-girl games trampled on people's lives. She was like a stampeding herd of horses, blindly crushing everything in her path. She was ten times more dangerous than a creature like Eros. At least he never intended harm, he was just reacting to his own fear. Alex calculatedly destroyed trust.

"Lose me?" He towered over her. "You never *had* me, lady!"

"Phillip."

He shook his head violently. "You're just like all the rest, aren't you, Alex Connelly? Or is your name even Alex?"

"It's still Alex. Short for Alexandra." Pride tinged her voice and brought up her tiny chin defiantly, but tears burned trails down the back of her throat.

"Well, Alexandra, I don't care to associate with people who find humor in hurting others. I'd appreciate it if you'd return to your brother. The two of you can have a good, long laugh at how successful your latest charade turned out."

"No! Oh, Phillip, it isn't…wasn't like that at all." Her emerald eyes pleaded with him.

"Goodbye, Alex."

She watched him walk away, her heart a throbbing lump in her throat, a wretched, hollow, hopeless feeling in her gut. She'd lost him, the one man who had ever, *would* ever make her feel special just for being Alex.

Not because she was Grant Connelly's daughter, an heiress, a jet-setter with a taste for adventure. With Phillip she
had just been herself, or as closely as possible to the self
she was just now discovering. She had been a woman who
loved horses, who wanted to write stories and who made
love in the most exquisite ways because she was *in love*
with the man in her bed.

Her man.

No, not any longer, she told herself. Phillip had rejected
her once and for all. How was she going to move on with
her life without him? She had no idea.

Eleven

Alex turned from the window of the villa at the sound of the telephone ringing. Her suitcases stood ready beside the foyer door. Phillip's driver had gone to bring the car to take her to the airport. She'd held out a fragile hope that Phillip might return to the house to at least say goodbye to her. But it seemed he intentionally was making himself scarce until she left.

Her heart ached at the thought of leaving him and Altaria.

Just as she picked up the phone, she caught a glimpse of Phillip crossing the yard between the two stables. He glanced once at the house. She held her breath. But he kept on walking and disappeared into the dark recesses of the nearest stable.

"Hello," she said over a horrid, stifling tightness in her lungs.

"That you, Alex?" a familiar voice asked.

"Drew?" She swiped at her eyes. It was her brother. "Are you in Chicago?"

"No, I've been in London, then Rome on business. Just wanted to see if I could catch you in Altaria before heading for home. I was surprised to find you weren't with Daniel at the palace. Are you all right?"

She forced lightness into her voice. "Of course I'm all right. When have I not been?" She'd left her fiancé the day before their wedding, had a blazing affair with a prince, who subsequently dropped her... Why shouldn't life be simply rosy? "As it turns out, I'm leaving for home tonight. Just waiting for my ride to the airport now."

"Oh, well, I guess I'll see you at the summer house when I get back. I'm wrapping things up early. I got a call from my daughter. Says she has a surprise for me, something very special, and she wants me home. Kids!" He sounded tickled to death with the summons from his little girl. Alex knew how much she meant to him.

"Sounds like a command performance before the queen. Guess you'd better not disappoint."

"I won't," he promised. Then the light tone of his voice altered. "I hear a lot's been going on at home. Pretty serious stuff, the investigation and all. Dad must be going out of his mind."

"We'll both have some catching up to do," she commented, although nothing seemed important anymore. Not now that Phillip had walked out of her life.

"See you back in Chi-town, sis," Drew said.

"Yes." Her stomach clenched, and she felt sickened by the thought.

She didn't want to leave Altaria, didn't want to return to her old life.

Didn't want to reenact all the old scenes with her friends and family. She couldn't be Alexandra, the party girl, the girl who would try anything once, then move on. She wanted permanency, a life that meant something. She wanted to be the woman she'd become in Phillip Kinrowan's arms.

Alex slowly let the telephone receiver rest in its cradle. She looked out the window. The driver had brought the car up to the front of the house, and Phillip was nowhere in sight.

Time to leave. Time to go home and try to figure out, once and for all, who she was meant to be.

Alex's heart felt lifeless. She couldn't even feel her own pulse. Her feet moved reluctantly across the rich Pasha carpet, as if literally weighed down by her remorse. The one man who had counted for anything, and she couldn't even be honest with him.

It might have worked. It might have been forever.

Phillip pitchforked fresh, sweet-smelling straw into Eros's stall after mucking it out. He worked fast and hard, intentionally trying to exhaust himself. If he bled himself of all energy, he wouldn't be able to think about Alex, wouldn't be able to remember the good times he now realized he'd subconsciously wished could go on forever.

In the background, beneath the sounds of the horses snuffling and shifting in their stalls, he heard a car engine growl to life, just as he felt his own will to endure seep away to nothingness. He closed his eyes. From the sounds, he could picture the vehicle pulling away from the front of the villa with Alex in it. Moving past the stables and driving off. The rumble of its engine faded to a hum, then was lost entirely among the softly comforting sounds of the horses.

She was gone. He hadn't looked up once, and he congratulated himself for being strong.

He wasn't sad, Phillip told himself. He was angry—and with good reason. Alex had played her selfish games, using him as a little child would use her dolls to act out dramas of her imagination. He doubted if even the tears she'd shed when he last saw her were real.

Alex had pretended for so long, she probably didn't know who she was or what she wanted. Hadn't he accused her of that? If only he'd listened to his own words. If only he'd remembered them and taken them to heart and not let her get under his skin as she had.

One thing was sure. He wasn't going to throw away his own life trying to figure out life for her.

He plunged the pitchfork into another pile of straw, then leaned on the handle and swore under his breath. Eros plodded over and nuzzled his cheek with a wet slobber.

"We won't miss her at all. Will we, boy?" Phillip muttered and stroked the gelding's silky neck. "Better off without her."

It was two weeks after Alex's return to Chicago, and life had returned to an all-too-familiar routine. She let herself be drawn in by her old friends. They whisked her off on unnecessary shopping trips, in search of clothing she didn't need, perfume that smelled like a funeral parlor and food that tasted like cardboard after the simple, sun-drenched delicacies of Altaria. She spent money because she was supposed to, not because there was anything she really wanted.

Long, dreary afternoons were spent at the spa, luxuriating in costly treatments to soothe her sun-pinked skin after her days of sailing and riding. But she felt worse rather than better.

She missed Phillip with all her heart and struggled to occupy herself, to forget a way of life that was honest and plain but exciting as long as it was with him. She could not forget. Everything around her appeared gray and felt boring after Altaria and Phillip.

One night she accepted an invitation to a party at a girlfriend's house. As soon as she walked in the door, she heard a voice she recognized. A lump of panic rose in her throat, and she spun around, searching desperately for the nearest escape route. Behind her was a door, and she didn't care where it led as long as it was out of the roomful of guests. She reached for the knob.

"Hey, you just got here," Sheila called from the middle of a well-heeled crowd, starting toward her.

Tonight, everyone wore black; it was the thing. Black with silver or platinum jewelry. The whole damn room looked as if they'd coordinated their clothing before dressing. Alex felt disgusted. Where had her head been when she'd chosen friends all these years? They were plastic replicas of real people, dressed up like mannequins.

"Where are you off to so fast?" Sheila bubbled.

"You didn't tell me Robert was coming," Alex said under her breath.

Sheila shrugged but didn't look at all guilty. "You didn't ask."

"Not funny." Alex turned toward the door again.

"Wait!" It wasn't Sheila's voice that stopped her, but Robert's.

She froze midstride, her blood running ice-cold through her body. She looked down at her hand without turning to face him. "There's nothing to say between us, Robert. You know that."

Sheila gave her a look that said she'd been in on the conspiracy. She ducked out of Robert's path and rejoined her other guests. Laughter, the clink of crystal, voices raised to be heard above the rising chatter, and Alex wished it would all go away.

"Alex, come on, please. Honey, you don't know how much I've missed you."

She looked at him for the first time in over a month. Robert Marsh was handsome in the expensive tuxedo obviously tailored just for him. His blond hair was trimmed perfectly, and his brown eyes sparkled with what she might have read as sincerity if she hadn't known better. Anyone observing them might have assumed he genuinely cared for her. But she had learned once, the hard way.

"Missed me, Robert? I doubt that. All you miss is your insurance policy."

"My what?"

"Me. Your security that your career will take you to the moon. Because you've married the boss's daughter."

He rolled his eyes, as if saying, *Women, what gets into them?* "You never gave me a chance to explain. I *love* you, Alex. You're more important to me than any job."

"I am?" Flashing her eyes at him, she stepped two degrees closer.

Alex poked him in the chest with one fingernail, perfectly shaped and lacquered a bloodred crimson. She hated the color, now that she thought about it. But it did make her feel just a little bit reckless, which was what she needed to get her through this final confrontation with Robert Marsh.

"You're certain I'm more important than your career?" she asked sweetly.

"Sure." He smiled, showing white teeth, but his eyes skittered around the room as if worried someone might overhear and refute him. "Working for Grant is just that— work. I thank God, though, I took that position with the company. If I hadn't I wouldn't have met you."

"Right." She didn't believe a word of it.

"So, what do you say, sweetheart? Can we get back together again? I mean, now that you've had time to cool off and—"

"Tell you what, Robert," she said cutting him off with a slashing movement of her hand. "I'll take you back on one condition."

He grinned, ecstatic at the possibility. "*Anything,* sweetheart, you name it!" His arm snaked around her waist, and she didn't fight him because she knew it wouldn't be there for long.

"Resign your position at Connelly Corporation, and promise me you'll never work for my family again."

His mouth literally dropped open. "Alex?"

"I mean it. If the job doesn't mean anything, walk away from it. We can live a simple life. We don't need a lot of money to be happy, do we, sweetheart?" She smiled at him coyly.

His arm fell away from her and he took a step backward. "I've worked hard to get where I am at Connelly. We'd have nothing."

"We'd have our love." It was a test, and it didn't matter if he knew it. She was sorry she didn't feel a thing for him when he hesitated for a moment longer, his face white, his lips pressed tightly together, the smiles gone. "That's all right, Robert. You don't have to say a thing. I know your answer."

She grasped his shoulders, easily turned him around and gave him a little shove to start him off. A moment later, he'd disappeared into the crowd, and she slipped out the door to her car. Sheila would be angry she'd ditched her party, but then again, she didn't think parties would matter much to her anymore. Not the kind her old friends gave. She no longer felt a part of their pointless lives.

Altaria in summer was more beautiful than any time during the year. Warm breezes off the Mediterranean, brilliant sunshine and afternoon showers lavished their attention on the lush tropical foliage and exotic blooms. The air was perfumed with their scent, and everywhere Phillip looked he saw evidence of the earth's generosity. He had always been content to be here, in this paradise. He should have been happy.

He was not. Alex had left him and his misery knew no bounds.

The perversity of it wasn't lost on him. She had left because he had told her she must, because he'd literally tossed her out. He'd done it because he believed he could only be happy without her. Only then would life make sense to him. But it didn't.

Barnaby Jacobs wasn't the first to point out how badly he'd handled things. Cook had scolded him for sulking. His stable master had said, "You didn't look so glum when the signorina was here." And even Dr. Elgado, whom he'd visited for his annual physical remarked that Phillip seemed unusually quiet and less interested in life.

They were right, dammit. But there was nothing he could do about it, was there? "After all," he confided in Barnaby one evening as they sat on his veranda, sharing cigars and a fine old port, "I'd just be asking for trouble, getting serious with a woman who can't tell the truth."

"You could look at it that way," Barnaby agreed. "Or you might see things differently."

"How differently?" Phillip growled.

"Well," Barnaby blew a silver-blue puff of smoke into the hazy night air, "there's a fine line between lying and being playful."

Phillip snorted. "Convincing the man you're with that you're someone you're not. You call that playful?"

"If she meant no harm in doing so, yes, I could see it that way."

Phillip took two hefty swallows of the port and let its rich warmth burn its way down his throat. "And how does one judge intent? She claims she wanted nothing from me, but it's never been true before. How can I believe this woman was so different?"

"Perhaps you just have to be a gambling man to appreciate a woman like Alex." Barnaby's trips to Monaco casinos were no secret.

"Gambling is a dangerous sport, solicitor."

"True. But sometimes the rewards are magnificent. I suppose it depends upon what's at stake. Many women, I suppose, wouldn't be worth the risk. But Alex... You know, Phillip, I don't think I can recall you smiling or laughing so much as when she was with you. You began to live again, really live. How is the boat coming, by the way?"

"Not badly," Phillip said, a note of pride in his voice. "I've nearly finished the rough plans. There is a shipyard in Nice that may be perfect for what I need. I'm flying there next week to meet with the naval architect and discuss details."

"That's wonderful. I think Alex would be very pleased to know this. She would be proud of you."

Phillip crushed out his half-smoked Havana in the crystal ashtray on the table before them. "There's no telling what that woman might think. She's a mystery."

"Aren't they all, in a way?"

"Not like Alex," Phillip grumbled.

Barnaby smiled. "No. She was truly special."

Phillip closed his eyes and remembered her as she'd stood by the roadside, astride Lucy, holding Eros's reins. She had sat so very tall in the saddle that day, giving him that impish grin that said she'd succeeded where all of his men had failed. Yet she had seemed so little, so fragile next to his horses.

Yes, he could imagine her being proud of him, returning to his dream.

"What about her, Phillip?"

"Hmmm?"

"Alex's dream. You said once that she considered writing fiction. Have you heard anything from her? Has she continued to write?"

"I don't know," he said, his voice sounding as hollow as his soul felt. "She hasn't tried to contact me. I don't expect she will, after the way we—" He couldn't go on.

"You miss her, don't you?" Barnaby laid a consoling hand over his arm.

"That's beside the point. I couldn't trust her."

Barnaby sighed. "Strange, I think she was the most honest woman I know."

Phillip laughed. "You've got to be kidding."

"Really. She knew the price she'd pay for telling you the truth. You told me after she left that she'd tried to say something to you earlier, but events kept getting in the way. That wasn't her fault. She must have loved you a great deal to be so afraid of telling you she was a Connelly and a member of the social elite you were so set on running away from.''

Phillip dropped his face into his hands and tried to make sense of it all. He had been so sure he was in the right. But now...now, the way his friend put it, the scale seemed to tip the other way.

"Even if I wanted her back in my life," he said slowly, "I'm pretty sure I've burned my bridges."

"Maybe not. Maybe there is some way you can show her you are a man who makes mistakes, a man who appreciates her."

He lifted his head and looked at the lawyer. "I can't begin to imagine a way to do that."

Barnaby blew a perfect smoke circle. It hovered for a moment in the still air, a silver ring that slowly drifted apart as a warm breeze caught it. "The right gift to go with the right promise. Something she can't buy for herself with her own money. Something that only you possess and can give to her. Something she loves."

Phillip blinked, thinking hard. There was one thing...

Emma Connelly did her best to comfort her daughter, but she wasn't successful. She felt for Alexandra. More than her other children, her daughter was fragile of spirit. She'd always tried too hard to please, searched too frantically for her place in life. Emma had hoped that marriage to a good young man would bring Alexandra the peace and joy Emma had come to know from her family. But Robert Marsh wasn't the right man for Alexandra.

And now, after returning from Altaria, her daughter seemed sadder than ever. But with the sadness there had come other changes. She seemed more sure of herself, less fragile. After the first week of meeting with old friends, she had set up a computer in her room and spent hours typing. Emma had seen some of the pages, and she was amazed at the joy and brilliance in her daughter's writing. It was as if she'd uncovered a hidden talent that had been waiting for just the right moment to show itself.

"Are you planning to write a book?" Emma had asked jokingly one afternoon.

Alexandra smiled a little, gave a sideways tilt to her head. "Maybe. I'll see."

Just like that. Perhaps there was hope for the girl yet. Emma only wished that finding herself hadn't cost her daughter so dearly. The man she'd met in Altaria, whose name was never spoken, had broken her heart if not her spirit. And that was a high price for finding oneself.

Alex finished typing the twentieth page of the day. Each morning she'd woken at seven sharp, and before breakfast had written at least five pages. She'd go for a walk, then return to her room, unable to keep her fingers from the keyboard. The story called to her.

On the day she reached the hundredth page, the housekeeper knocked on her door. "Package for you, miss."

"Leave it on the bed, Ruby. I'll open it later," she said absently.

The woman peeked into the room. "I don't think I can do that, Ms. Alexandra."

Alex turned to face her, but the woman covered a smile with her hand and ducked out of the room. What had gotten into Ruby?

"Well, leave it in the foyer, and I'll—"

"Mrs. Connelly would never allow that," Ruby called back up the stairs at her.

Alex sighed. What the devil—?

She saved her file on the computer and shut down the program, knowing she'd written herself out for the day. Tomorrow, she promised herself, she would finish that chapter and start the next. The book was becoming more and more real every day. She felt such jubilation at the completion of each scene. Yet when she stopped writing she had to face the rest of her life, and the knowledge that some power beyond her understanding had determined that it would be a lonely existence without the man she loved.

She walked down the stairs from her room and into the foyer, looking for the package that Ruby had said was delivered. There was no box of any sort to be seen. Had the woman really meant it couldn't be brought inside? She opened the door and stepped outside, looking to one side then the other of the door. Nothing stood on the porch but the familiar wicker furniture.

"Over here," a voice called.

She looked up, expecting to see a delivery truck. An immense ebony horse stood in the grass circle in the center of the drive; its reins were held by a man. A man who shouldn't have been where he was.

Alex put a hand out and steadied herself against the door jamb. "Phillip."

He started walking Eros toward her. "I told the woman who answered the door that I expected your delivery should wait outside."

She choked on a bubble of laughter. "Mother would be a little dismayed to find that creature in her foyer." Then her smile left, and in place of it she felt the coldness sweep over her again. "What's this all about, Phillip? I did what you asked of me. I left. But we can't be friends, not after what we had back in Altaria."

"That's too bad," he said. "I would like you as a friend."

She shook her head. Her throat spasmed, and her eyes burned with tears she refused to let fall. "That would be too hard, to just be pals."

"Then I suppose we'd better be more than that." He stopped in front of her and handed her Eros's reins. "Here, my peace offering."

"You flew him all the way to the States to give to me?" She was astonished.

"I was wrong, Alex. I love you. I shouldn't have run you off the way I did. I want you in my life."

The words sang in her soul. "But can you trust me now?"

"I'll trust you to keep me interested in life. To keep me guessing, and encourage me to do the things I once loved and still dream of doing."

"Your boat," she whispered.

"I'm working on it. We go into production next month, if all goes well."

"Oh, Phillip, really? That's wonderful."

"But it won't mean anything to me if you're not there with me."

She looked down at her hands. "You might change your mind. You might tell me to leave again. I couldn't bear that."

"I won't. Here, hop aboard. Let's go for a ride and talk."

He mounted the big horse and reached down for her.

She hesitated but at last gave him her hand, and he pulled her up behind him. She squirmed on the back half of the saddle.

"It's not very comfortable. There's something lumpy back here."

"Oh really? Must be a burr or something. Better check it out."

She slid back on Eros's rump, pulled up the leather flap and reached under carefully. Her fingertips hit something soft, and she pulled it out.

"It looks like a little velvet pouch of some kind."

"Huh," he grunted and started Eros moving away from the house, down the long gravel drive. "Fancy that. What's in it?"

"I don't know." She gripped the horse with her knees to keep from sliding off as his easy gait took them slowly toward the side gardens. Her fingers pulled at the silk cords, and she reached inside. A warm circle of gold came out with her fingers. A diamond glittered up at her.

"Oh!"

"Did something bite you?"

"Oh, Phillip, you're wonderful!"

He chuckled. "Guess not."

She was about to punch him for his wisecrack, when he lifted one leg over Eros's head and slid to the ground. He took the ring from her and reached up to slip it over the appropriate finger. "Marry me, Alex. Pretend you love me, if you don't. Pretend you want to be my wife, my mate, my lover, my friend and companion forever. Pretend anything you like, but first these things then don't ever stop using your imagination. And I promise I'll love you forever and never again turn you away."

She was weeping as the gold band slipped up her finger. Weeping for joy.

"Crocodile tears?" he asked.

She shook her head, unable to speak. "No. Real. Yes, yes, Phillip. I'll be all those things." She kissed him on his upturned mouth. "But I don't need to pretend anymore. I'll let my characters do the pretending from here on."

"Good," he said. "Then I won't have to worry about your faking certain reactions, will I?"

She laughed at the wicked gleam in his eyes. "You never had to worry about that, my love."

"Good." He pulled her down from the saddle and wrapped his arms around her. "Now let's go tell your parents that there's going to be a wedding after all."

And this time, with the right groom, she thought jubilantly.

*   *   *   *   *

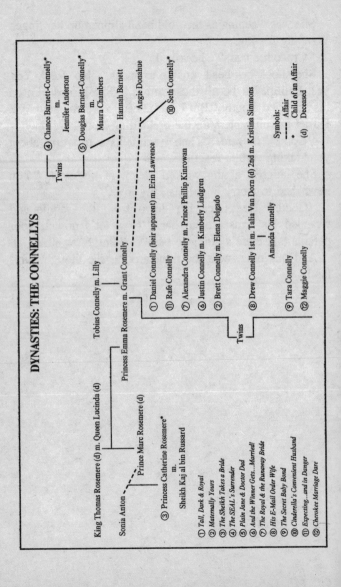

DYNASTIES: THE CONNELLYS

King Thomas Rosemere (d) m. Queen Lucinda (d)

Tobias Connelly m. Lilly

Sonia Anton

Prince Marc Rosemere (d)

Princess Emma Rosemere m. Grant Connelly

Chance Barnett-Connelly*
m.
Jennifer Anderson

Douglas Barnett-Connelly*
m.
Maura Chambers

Twins

④ Chance Barnett-Connelly*
⑤ Douglas Barnett-Connelly*

Hannah Barnett

Angie Donahue

⑩ Seth Connelly*

③ Princess Catherine Rosemere*
m.
Sheikh Kaj al bin Russard

① Daniel Connelly (heir apparent) m. Erin Lawrence

⑪ Rafe Connelly

⑦ Alexandra Connelly m. Prince Phillip Kinrowan

⑥ Justin Connelly m. Kimberly Lindgren

② Brett Connelly m. Elena Delgado

⑧ Drew Connelly 1st m. Talia Van Dorn (d) 2nd m. Kristina Simmons

Amanda Connelly

Twins

⑨ Tara Connelly

⑫ Maggie Connelly

① Tall, Dark & Royal
② Maternally Yours
③ The Sheikh Takes a Bride
④ The SEAL's Surrender
⑤ Plain Jane & Doctor Dad
⑥ And the Winner Gets…Married!
⑦ The Royal & the Runaway Bride
⑧ His E-Mail Order Wife
⑨ The Secret Baby Bond
⑩ Cinderella's Convenient Husband
⑪ Expecting…and in Danger
⑫ Cherokee Marriage Dare

Symbols:
- - - Affair
• Child of an Affair
(d) Deceased

One

Drew Connelly dropped his bags at the bottom of the staircase leading to the second floor—and landed the largest on his foot. He muttered a string of curses directed at his stupidity, the late hour, the sound of the new nanny's grating voice coming from the kitchen while she gabbed on the phone with God only knew who.

If he hadn't been desperate, he'd never have left Debbie in charge of Amanda while he'd tended urgent business in Europe.

God, how he'd missed his daughter. A month was entirely too long to be away from her. The daily phone calls had been sorry replacements for seeing her vibrant smile, hearing her contagious laughter. Amanda was the very light of his life, and the reason why he got up every morning to face his grueling schedule as vice president of Overseas Operations for Connelly Corporation, his family's legacy.

Unfortunately, the responsibility was rapidly aging him. Tonight he felt two-hundred years old, not twenty-seven.

Trudging up the stairs, Drew planned to immediately go to Mandy's room and kiss her good-night, take a quick shower, then pass out in bed. But he stopped short when he heard a giggle coming from his study. Amanda's giggle.

So much for his daughter being tucked soundly into bed.

Drew dropped his bags once again, this time avoiding his toes, and strode down the hallway and into the office to find Amanda perched on her knees in his chair, her face lit by the glow of the computer screen and sheer amusement.

"Young lady, you're supposed to be in bed," he said with all the sternness he could muster. Which wasn't much.

"Daddy! You're home!" Amanda climbed out of the chair and rushed him like a tiny tornado. Drew hoisted her up in his arms, relishing the clean scent of her hair, her soft cheek resting against his evening-shadowed jaw.

After he hugged her hard and kissed her cheek, she pulled back and studied him with green eyes bright with excitement. "Daddy, I missed you so bad!"

"I missed you, too, sweetheart. But haven't I told you that you're not supposed to be on the Internet unless an adult is with you? It's dangerous, Mandy."

"I know, Daddy." She began to play with his tie, avoiding his scrutiny. "But Nana Lilly was with me before and Debbie just left. We were surfing together."

That provided little relief for Drew. "Visiting your favorite animal site?"

"I helped Debbie pick out a man."

"What do you mean you picked out a man?"

"On *Singlemania*. The same place we got your surprise."

The scenario was getting more and more bizarre. "My surprise?"

His daughter's face once again brightened. "The surprise I told you about on the phone, silly Daddy. Nana helped me get it. It will be here in the morning."

Drew sensed certain disaster. Nothing good could come from a singles' Web site. He wasn't even sure he wanted to know what his daughter had done, but he had to find out. "What kind of surprise did you and Nana come up with?"

She looked away again. "I'm not supposed to tell you cause then it won't be a surprise."

"Ah, come on, Mandy," he cajoled. "Just a little hint. I won't tell Nana you told me."

Amanda tipped up her chin with pride, beamed like a billboard, and proudly announced, "We got you a wife."

*   *   *   *   *

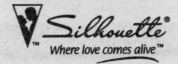

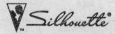

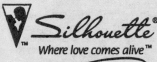

COMING NEXT MONTH

#1453 BECKETT'S CINDERELLA—Dixie Browning
Man of the Month/Beckett's Fortune
Experience had taught Liza Chandler not to trust handsome men with
money. Then unbelievably sexy Beckett Jones strolled into her life and set
her pulse racing. Liza couldn't deny that he seemed to be winning the battle
for her body, but would he also win her heart?

#1454 HIS E-MAIL ORDER WIFE—Kristi Gold
Dynasties: The Connellys
Tycoon Drew Connelly was unprepared for the sizzling attraction
between him and Kristina Simmons, the curvaceous bride his daughter
and grandmother had picked for him from an Internet site. Though he
didn't intend to marry her, his efforts to persuade Kristina of that fact
backfired. But her warmth and beauty tempted him, and soon he found
himself yearning to claim her....

#1455 FALLING FOR THE ENEMY—Shawna Delacorte
Paige Bradford thought millionaire Bryce Lexington was responsible for
her father's misfortune, and she vowed to prove it—by infiltrating his
company. But she didn't expect that her sworn enemy's intoxicating kisses
would make her dizzy with desire. Was Bryce really a ruthless shark, or
was he the sexy and honorable man she'd been searching for all her life?

#1456 MILLIONAIRE COP & MOM-TO-BE—Charlotte Hughes
When wealthy cop Neil Logan discovered that beautiful Katie Jones
was alone and pregnant, he proposed a marriage of convenience. But
make-believe romance soon turned to real passion, and Neil found himself
falling for his lovely bride. Somehow, he had to show Katie that he could
love, honor and cherish her—forever!

#1457 COWBOY BOSS—Kathie DeNosky
Cowboy Cooper Adams was furious when an elderly matchmaker hired
Faith Broderick as his housekeeper without his permission—and then
stranded them on his remote ranch. Cooper didn't have time for romance,
yet he had to admit that lovely Faith aroused primitive stirrings, and
promoting her from employee to wife would be far too easy to do....

#1458 DESPERADO DAD—Linda Conrad
A good man was proving hard to find for Randi Cullen. Then FBI agent
Manuel Sanchez appeared and turned her world upside down. He proposed
a marriage of convenience so he could keep his cover, and Randi happily
accepted. But Randi was tired of being a virgin, so she had to find a way to
convince Manuel that she truly wanted to be his wife—in *every* way!

SDCNM0702